Long Road to Revenge

A stage coach is robbed, and there are no witnesses; every soul who was aboard is missing or dead. With his sister among those who were killed, Cole Garvin swears he'll not rest until those responsible are six feet under. He's not the only one seeking out the murderers, but it's hard to know who can be trusted.

Tracking down a gang of ruthless outlaws is no job for a peace-loving rancher, and Garvin leaves his scruples behind to take up the way of the gun. When he meets a special lady it's just too bad; there's no time for love on the road to revenge.

By the same author

Hang the Sheriff High
Nemesis Trail
Ride Back to Redemption
Hideout
A Place Called Jeopardy

Long Road to Revenge

Eugene Clifton

A Black Horse Western

ROBERT HALE · LONDON

ISBN 978-0-7090-8704-5

Robert Hale Limited
Clerkenwell House
Clerkenwell Green
London EC1R 0HT

www.halebooks.com

*To Blue, Harvey and all the other horses down the years.
Faithful friends and the best of company.*

Typeset by
Derek Doyle & Associates, Shaw Heath
Printed and bound in Great Britain by
CPI Antony Rowe, Wiltshire

CHAPTER ONE

'I thought the stage was due at 11.15.' A tall figure in worn chaps and battered Stetson pushed away from the wall of the Wells Fargo office, to confront the man who appeared in the doorway.

'You're not wrong, mister.' The clerk looked hot, though he was in shirtsleeves and had discarded his vest. He had to tilt his head quite a way to meet the stranger's eyes; he took in the open expression of a man who didn't have a care in the world, and grunted, jamming a narrow-brimmed hat down to his ears. With a harassed look the clerk set off, almost trotting along the sidewalk, the long-legged stranger striding easily along beside him.

The man from the Wells Fargo office slowed down a little. 'Something I can do for you?' he enquired irritably.

'Not unless you happen to know why the stage is nearly three hours late,' the man replied cheerfully, and the clerk came to a halt, turning to face him, a deep sigh escaping from his down-turned mouth, followed by a flood of words, as if the sigh had marked the opening of a dam.

'I don't, and that's a fact. It's a worry, mister, because she's never been this much overdue, and it's only a four-hour run from the overnight way station. She's scheduled to leave at 7.15, and Joe out there's a real stickler for keeping to time. He would have sent word with a rider if the stage hadn't got in last night, and if there was trouble this morning they've had time to get somebody to town twice over. Sure will be good if they got the telegraph out here. Small town like Sykes' Pass gets overlooked, that's the trouble.'

Without, apparently, pausing to take a breath he was back in motion, angling across the street, the lanky cowboy beside him. 'Could just be a busted spring, but I'm afraid somebody will have to go out and take a look, and I'm not supposed to leave town. You got folks expected?'

The torrent came to a stop so abruptly that the stranger took a moment to realize he was supposed to make an answer. 'My sister's coming from back East,' he said. 'Haven't seen her in a long time. I'd thought of going to fetch her myself, but I'd heard the route from Indian Falls to Dobie's Bluff was real safe these days.'

'Local Indians haven't given us no trouble this last five years,' the clerk confirmed. He shook his head. 'That's why I've got nobody to send; those bosses back in their big fancy offices reckon it's all nice and civilized around these parts. But a horse can still pull up lame, or a wheel come off, and who has to sort it out? Me, that's who.'

'If there's anything I can do, I'm ready and willing,' the cowboy said. 'Got a horse at the livery across the street.'

'Well, if you don't want to wait around till Mike gets back, I reckon he won't argue with taking along some company, he'd probably be obliged to you. That's if I can persuade him to get his backside out of his chair.'

'Mike? Is that the marshal?' the stranger asked, reading the sign on the door in front of them.

'That's right. Mike Tate.' The Wells Fargo man dived

6

into the marshal's office. 'Mike, the 11.15 didn't get in. Never been more than an hour late since they started the route. You know that, regular as clockwork, even when the weather's bad, which it isn't. There's maybe a horse gone lame, though if Bert's driving he's a good man, he's brought her in with only three pulling and still only been thirty minutes behind schedule, and you know Joe, he would've sent word if there was something wrong at his end. I was wondering if you'd mind doing me a favour, take a ride out and see if there's some problem.'

The marshal was a compact man, greying at the temples. He leant back in his swivel chair and looked up at the clerk, his eyes bright blue beneath bushy eyebrows. 'Slow down, Clive. Try saying that again so a man can get to hear it.' Before the Wells Fargo man could speak, the marshal noticed the stranger who stood in the doorway. 'Something I can do for you?'

'My business is the same as his,' the tall man replied, tipping a thumb at the clerk as he swept his battered hat from his head with the other hand. 'Name's Cole Garvin. Came into town to meet my sister off the Indian Falls stage, but I hear it's over three hours late. Clive here suggested you might be taking a ride out that way, and if that's so I was hoping you wouldn't object to some company.'

The marshal looked Garvin up and down, seeing a man of maybe thirty years or so, his complexion well-weathered by a life spent out of doors. A pair of quiet dark eyes met his in a level gaze that spoke of an easy self-assurance. Garvin's mouth curved in a half-smile at the marshal's scrutiny; there was a humorous warmth in them as he made his own appraisal of the lawman. Tate nodded a slow approval, liking what he saw. Unlike the clerk, here was a

7

man who would only speak when he had something to say, and what he said would probably be worth hearing.

'Fine. Guess the two of us will have to make up the search party, seeing Clive here never did learn to sit a horse.'

'That's not true, Marshal,' the clerk blustered, though the reddening of his face gave him away. 'I'm supposed to stay around the office. I'd be in trouble if I left it. Besides, you know what the doctor said about my back . . .'

'Sure, it don't matter none,' Tate said, laughing as he lifted a hand to silence the little man. 'Go back to your office and shuffle your papers; we'll go find the stage for you. Come on, mister, you look like you're used to the saddle anyways.'

'Rode nearly two days to get here,' the tall man affirmed. 'Don't come this way often, I do my trading at River Bend.'

'And the stage don't call there,' the marshal said. 'Meeting your sister, did you say? Be a long ride back for a woman.'

'I've got a new rig ordered from the feller at the end of Main Street, he said it'd be ready tomorrow. Reckon to drive my sister back home in style, and pick up a few stores at the same time.'

Five minutes later the two men rode out on the east-bound road, their horses settling into an easy lope. They didn't speak much as the dusty miles passed beneath the horses' hoofs, riding in a companionable silence. They had covered half the distance to the way station when the marshal suddenly leant forward, squinting into the heat haze. 'You see something up ahead?'

For answer, Cole Garvin clapped spurs to his horse's flanks, and they raced side by side towards the dark shape that shimmered on the road up ahead.

The coach stood empty, with no sign of the four horses that had brought it this far. Circling warily, the marshal rode wide around the abandoned vehicle, alternately scanning the ground and the surrounding country. Garvin lit down, ground reined his mount and peered in through the open door. 'There's blood here,' he called. Testing the stain on the seat with a finger he found it was bone dry. 'Not much, and hours old,' he declared, as Marshal Tate rode back to join him.

'I've found signs that a bunch of horses went south, five, maybe six hours ago,' the marshal said. 'Looks like two riders were waiting, hiding behind that outcrop. Assuming it was a hold-up they took quite a risk, there's always a shotgun rides this route, and if Bert was driving he'd be carrying his own scatter-gun.'

'No sign of any weapons in here,' Garvin said, peering around the inside of the coach. 'No spent cartridges either.'

The marshal tethered his horse to the coach and climbed up to the box. 'Nor here. Guess they didn't get a chance to make a fight of it. Mail's gone. Hard to tell whether they were carrying anything else worth stealing. Guess Clive will know.' The marshal stood on the roof of the coach and scanned the horizon. 'Don't make sense. Driver, guard, maybe three or four passengers. Where'd they go?'

Garvin's face was grim beneath the dusty, battered Stetson. 'Any sign that there were people on foot along with the horses?'

'Hard to tell. You figure they kidnapped the passengers? Why the heck would they do that? Sure would slow 'em down.' Marshal Tate shook his head, grimacing.

9

'Sorry, Mr Garvin. For your sister's sake I hope I'm wrong, but I reckon we'll find them around here someplace. Keep your eyes open for vultures, they'll spot 'em sooner than we will.' He climbed down and untied his horse. 'I'll take this side of the road, you take the other.'

It wasn't vultures that led Garvin to the heap of rocks nearly a mile from the trail, but a dozen crows, protesting noisily as they rose into the air at his approach. His horse smelled the blood before he did, throwing its head up and snorting uneasily. He soothed the beast with hand and voice, wrinkling his nose as the sickly scent of death filled his nostrils, a cold, hard knot forming somewhere under his ribs.

A single shot from his gun brought the marshal. They took their horses upwind a little and tied them to a dead tree.

The two bodies lay face down, side by side. There was a small blackened hole in the back of each man's vest, dead centre, sparsely fringed with dried blood. 'That's Bert Calloway,' the marshal said, tight jawed. 'He was driving. Don't know the other man, but I'd guess he was riding shotgun.'

'He's dressed more like a drummer.' Garvin bent to check the dead man's pockets. He came upright holding two pieces of card. 'Joel Taylor, purveyor of fine fabrics and ladies' haberdashery,' he read. 'And this one's a ticket for the westbound stage. He was a passenger.'

'So, what happened to the shotgun? Unless that explains why there was only two of them needed to carry out the hold-up,' Tate said thoughtfully. 'Be a whole lot easier to stop the stage if they'd got their own man riding on the box.'

'Why leave these two right out here? Why not shoot

10

them back there by the coach?'

'Buying time. They knew it would take us a while to find them,' The marshal's expression was grim. 'And we know for a fact there's at least one passenger missing. Could be there's more to find.'

Garvin met his look, his eyes hard and cold. 'Nothing we can do for these two, we have to keep searching.' Lifting back into the saddle, he scanned the scuffed ground. 'There's got to be some sign.'

'There's just a chance they took your sister along,' Tate said, seeing from the other man's look that this wasn't much comfort. Garvin was barely recognizable as the smiling stranger who'd drifted into his office a few hours ago; his face was all angles, his dark eyes like obsidian chips.

'I'm sorry,' the marshal went on, 'I need to get back to town. Takes a while to put together a posse. If they have taken her, we don't want to waste time. Young, is she?'

'Just nineteen. And pretty.' Garvin said bleakly. 'Reckon maybe I'll stay a while. It was crows showed me the way here. They headed that way, quite a bunch of them.' He waved a hand to the south, even further from the trail. 'I'll go take a look.'

The marshal hesitated a moment then nodded. 'All right, count me in. Another hour won't make much difference. We'll still be back in town before dark, and I can have the posse out here by first light.'

Marshal Tate spurred along a shallow gully, leaving Garvin to search among a desolate area of broken stone. Watching his horse's ears, the tall cowboy moved out to the windward side; the beast would let him know if it scented blood again.

'Here.' Tate's voice echoed across the distance between them. Something in the tone of that one word said it all, and Garvin raked his spurs savagely against his mount's sides. Unused to such treatment the horse leapt forward, squealing a protest.

Mike Tate turned his mount so it barred the other man's way. 'Reckon you need to take a breath or two before you see this,' he said softly. The dark eyes bored into his for a second, then Garvin gave a brief nod of his head, jerked at his rein and rode around him.

He knew her at once, though it had been two years. The girl he remembered, barely more than a child when they last met, lay half-naked, dead and defiled, her blood blackening the dust.

She'd been left in a shallow scrape, almost as if somebody had started to dig her grave. Her dark hair was loose, obscuring most of her face. That seemed a kindness, one not extended to the pale swell of her naked breasts, exposed to the sun and the dust, the white lace-trimmed blouse she had worn ripped to shreds, and stippled with brown stains. Garvin's gaze travelled relentlessly on, taking in what lay half-hidden by the ruin of her skirt. A deep shudder passed through him.

The marshal came to lay a blanket over her, but Garvin stopped him, laying a hand on the lawman's arm before he covered the girl's face.

'I swear, Julie,' he said, his voice as cold and unforgiving as a midwinter frost, 'I won't go home until the men who did this are dead and buried. I'll see them pay the price for what they've done, or I'll die trying.'

CHAPTER TWO

Dobie's Bluff was brimful, its streets overflowing with wagons and horses that were packed so thick it was hard to make a way through. Miners, wranglers, trappers, ranch hands, bagmen and two-bit gamblers had come from miles around, jostling elbows with the townsfolk because the rodeo was in town.

For the most part the crowd was good-tempered; it was early in the day and the serious drinking hadn't got started. A tall, lean man in a battered Stetson pushed his way between a couple of drifters.

'Hey!' One of them made to swing a fist in protest, but his companion grabbed his arm.

'C'mon, Harry,' he said, 'we gotta get to the corral while there's still some places.'

'That galoot trod on my foot,' Harry complained, but he allowed himself to be pulled away; a chill seemed to surround the lanky stranger, the man's eyes were cold and unforgiving, like chips of stone, and his lips were drawn into a thin hard line.

Cole Garvin had barely seen the two drifters. In fact he hardly noticed the crowds seething around him. He was intent on reaching the sheriff's office, his height allowing him to locate the building across the heads of the heaving mass of humanity filling the street. Although he was walking against the tide, which was aiming for the corral, some instinct caused men to move aside as he thrust unheeding through their midst.

'Somethin' I can do for you?' The sheriff barely glanced in the stranger's direction. He stood by his desk, buckling on his gun belt. 'Only I'm kinda busy.'

'Name's Cole Garvin. I'm looking for somebody.' Garvin reached into his pocket and took out a crumpled piece of paper.

'Mister, I got no time for bounty hunters,' the lawman said coldly. 'You'll find the door behind you. I'd advise you to clear out of my town, and count yourself lucky I got a lot on my mind right now, else I might just find a reason to put you behind bars.'

'Far as I know the men I'm looking for aren't wanted by the law. And just for the record, I've got no interest in bounty money. All I aim to do is ask them a few questions.' He had the paper unfolded, and held it out to the sheriff. 'Any of those names familiar to you?'

'I'd need to have a good reason for answerin' a question like that,' the sheriff said, making no move to take the paper. His tone was mild, though there was steel in his eyes.

Garvin nodded. 'I have a reason. Those people were on a westbound stage, due to reach Dobie's Bluff nearly two months ago.'

'Two months?' The sheriff stared at the stranger, taking in his appearance for the first time. The man was so lean he was hardly more than skin and bone; he had thinned down to a tough well-seasoned core. Whatever it was that drove him, he looked as if he would endure long after

14

other men had given up. 'If these folks were passin' through I reckon they'll be long gone, mister.'

'They've got to have come from somewhere, Dobie's Bluff is as good a place to start as any.' Again Garvin proffered the list. 'Don't mean to inconvenience you none. All I'm asking is that you take a look, see if there's anyone here you recognize.'

'If that's what it takes to get you off my back.' Reluctantly the sheriff took the paper and scanned it. 'How come you got some of these names crossed out? You already find those people?'

'In a manner of speaking. They're dead. And before you ask, I had nothing to do with their deaths.'

The sheriff looked again at the list, and a sudden understanding lit his eyes. 'Bert Calloway. He was drivin' that stage from Indian Falls, the one that was held up and robbed. I heard he got shot. These others, were they all passengers?'

'Last one, Zeke Dailey, he was riding shotgun, but seems he was in cahoots with the gang, so it's likely that wasn't his rightful name. Aside from him, those are the names Wells Fargo had for the folk who bought tickets. You'll see there are two men unaccounted for. It's possible one of them was involved in the robbery as well, since their bodies weren't found. That's what I'm trying to find out.'

'You left it too long to come searching. Assuming you can prove one of these men was involved, he could be in Mexico by now.'

'I don't think so. I didn't get here sooner because I was riding with Marshal Tate from Sykes' Pass. The posse were on the heels of at least four men, followed them for weeks. Got fooled now and then when they laid a false trail, but we kept a tag on them all the way to Silver Crossing. That's

15

where the trail finally went cold. So, they could be a week or more ahead of me, but I figure I'll pick them up again in time. Dobie's Bluff's the sort of place they might go to ground, and it's not more than a two-day ride from Silver Crossing if a man's in a hurry. Figure they must have some good reason for sticking to this part of the country.'

'Why you so sure this Dailey was involved with the gang?' The sheriff tapped a finger on the paper.

'Because the man who was supposed to ride shotgun went missing the night before the stage was due to leave.' Garvin explained. 'He's never been found. Dailey had drifted into town a couple of days before, made himself useful doing odd jobs at the depot, and when the regular shotgun didn't turn up he offered to take his place. I reckon his name could be Zeke right enough, I asked around town and everyone agreed he answered to it like it was his own, but I got my doubts about him owning up to Dailey. Marshal Tate figures he bushwhacked the man who was due to ride the stage that day; river's handy and it runs deep through there, real easy way to get rid of a dead man.'

'Sounds possible,' the sheriff conceded, scanning the paper again then looking up abruptly, his brows furrowed. 'What did you say your name was?'

'Garvin. Cole Garvin.'

'This woman, she'd be your wife maybe?'

'My sister.' The tall man bit off the words, his expression grim.

The lawman gave a slow nod. 'Guess that explains why you're here.' He went back to looking at the list. 'I heard there were three people killed, but you got four names crossed out.'

'The posse found the fourth about six days out from

where the stage was stopped. He was a rancher, Willard Simons. You must have known him, Sheriff, his spread's not that far from here.'

'You mean Will Simons from the Circle S? Hell, Will's dead?' the sheriff shook his head. 'Don't that beat all. I never knew his name was Willard.'

'He died of a bullet in the gut, but not before they'd given him a real hard time.' Garvin's face was drawn into tight lines. 'These men evidently have a liking for seeing folks suffer. Trouble is, nobody seems to know much about these other two passengers. Could be they were all in on the robbery, or maybe some were taken along for the ride, like Simons, to give these bastards some entertainment. I answered your questions, Sheriff, how about you see if you can answer mine?'

The sheriff nodded. 'Not much I can tell you.' He pondered a moment. 'There's a man by the name of Hollick come for the rodeo, ask anybody, can't barely miss hearin' it. He's the crazy cuss who'll be ridin' that mad stallion King Mo's got down there. One thing though. I can't recall his first name, but it ain't Tom.' He held the list out to hand it back.

'What about the other one?' Garvin asked, not taking the proffered paper. 'Man I talked to at the livery seemed to think you might know Josiah Marriday.'

The sheriff looked down at the list yet again. 'Marriday. Hell yes. There's an old-timer spends his time hangin' around these parts, takes a job for a few days when he has to, but mostly just bums drinks in the rougher saloons downtown. Everybody calls him Maddy, but I got a feelin' I heard somewhere that his name was Marriday. I don't recall seein' him in Dobie's Bluff since last fall. Anyway, what would a no-hoper like Maddy be doin' on a stage?

17

Anytime he's got a dollar in his pocket it goes straight down his throat.'

'According to the clerk at the depot at Indian Flats, one of the passengers was an old man with white hair down to his shoulders. Does that fit?'

'Sounds like Maddy.' The sheriff nodded. 'Real strange though. If he wanted to get out of Indian Flats he'd hitch a ride on a chuck wagon or somethin', not buy a ticket for the stage. Reckon maybe somebody made a mistake.'

'I'd still like to check it out. You know if he's got any place to call home in these parts?' Garvin asked.

'He used to work a stretch of the river for gold once, long time back. Reckon he might still have a shack out there.' The sheriff turned to the map that was hanging behind his desk. 'You know how to figure one of these?'

'Near enough,' Garvin replied.

The street was almost empty. 'They'll all be down at the corral by now,' the sheriff said, as the two men took to the sidewalk. 'There's been a lot of talk about this black stallion. Seems it nearly killed a wrangler last week, I'd guess it's the biggest draw King Mo ever had. Reckon I know where we can get us a view, if you're interested.'

Garvin shrugged. 'I won't get a chance to talk to this man Hollick until after his ride. Might as well take a look.' He followed where the sheriff led, up an outside stair and across a roof. The rising tide of sound from the crowds grew louder as they jumped over a narrow alleyway, ten foot above the ground, and scaled another ridge.

'Best seat in the house,' the sheriff said, making himself comfortable astride the ridge on the rooftop. The building overlooked the corral, and they had the place to themselves. 'Just in time. There's the man you're looking for,

18

the one with the gold bandanna.'

Three men were holding the black stallion down as it attempted to climb out of the chute. One of the wranglers, a large man with a hatchet face, had hold of the rope twisted round the animal's neck and was tightening it savagely. A fourth man, the one wearing the bright-yellow neckerchief, came climbing across the top of the chute to slam his fist on the big man's arm, shouting something that was lost in the general clamour. With a shrug the wrangler slackened his hold, and the newcomer stood poised, waiting for the right moment to lower himself into the saddle. 'You say that's Hollick?' Garvin asked.

'That's him. Supposed to be some fancy rider, but he's not so young now, the bets are spread pretty even.'

The cowboy looked up suddenly, and Garvin got a glimpse of a square jawed face and light-coloured eyes. Raising a hand, the man waved to somebody across the ring, where a barn made up one side of the enclosure. There were dozens of people sitting precariously on the steep-pitched roof, but two boys had the best position, right at the front and in the middle. The smaller youngster waved in reply, just as the man let himself on to the horse's back. With a taut grin that was more like a grimace, the rider gave a signal, and the door of the chute was flung open. A deafening yell from the watching crowd filled the air, echoing off the wall of the barn, as the stallion exploded into the dusty arena.

The animal gave a series of spine jarring bucks, then it leapt forward as if intent on dashing itself against the worn planks of the barn wall. In an amazing show of strength and skill Hollick dragged its head around, and the horse skidded, almost falling on its side, one knee scraping the ground before it came upright. Again it tried the same

19

manoeuvre, and again it was brought up short, this time with its head only inches away from the crowd lining the railings.

'Is he supposed to ride that thing to a standstill?' Garvin asked, having to shout to make himself heard.

'That's the idea,' came the reply. 'Some horse, huh?' The sheriff was leaning forward, adding his voice to the rest. 'C'mon, Hollick, I got twenty bucks ridin' on you!'

'That horse is crazy,' Garvin said. The animal stood tossing its head briefly, eyes rolling, before it launched itself forward in another attempt to plough into the crowd.

'What? Sure, it's real mad.' The lawman grinned. 'Don't reckon to humans much.'

'I don't mean that. There's something wrong in its head. You only have to look at it.'

For a third, a fourth time, the stallion tried to gallop its way out of the corral, seeming unaware that it was imprisoned between the four wooden walls. Continuously shaking its head, sometimes the animal bared its teeth and lunged at the air, as if it saw invisible enemies, then it would give a few more bone jarring bucks, snorting in rage.

Hollick was tiring. His lips were drawn back in a desperate grimace, his teeth clenched. The horse swung round to face the barn again. With a scream that could be heard clear above the animal howls issuing from several hundred human throats, it flung its head down and put all its strength into one last bid to run.

The man in the saddle was jerked forward, his balance gone. The slightest sideways move would have thrown him off, but the horse seemed to have forgotten that it bore a rider. With a massive thrust from its quarters the stallion catapulted directly at the barn wall.

Silence fell, every man abruptly holding his breath. Hollick made a last heave on the rope and brought the horse's head up, so that its legs struck the wall first, then the force of the impact sent the rider shooting forward. A few inches either way and he'd have hit the shingles. Instead, his head thudded into a massive timber jutting out, an eight-inch log that supported the roof of the barn. The man's body rebounded, flopping back into the saddle.

Despite its front legs being mangled at every move, the stallion was still trying to push its way through the half-rotten planks. Up on the roof men were yelling as they tried to scramble clear; the building was shaking and the steep pitch threatened to throw them down into the corral. The two boys, wide-eyed, didn't move. As the horse continued its frenzied attempt to escape from the madness that hazed its brain, blood spraying from its injuries, they sat staring down at the man sagging limply in the saddle.

CHAPTER THREE

Panic broke out on the roof. As men fought to get away from the edge, one of them fell into the corral, to land only a yard from the thrashing body of the stallion, still held bizarrely upright by the splintered timbers which had pierced its body as it lunged into the side of the barn. The sheriff was on his feet, staring across at the chaos. 'Holy Moses.'

His face devoid of emotion, Garvin drew his .45 and took aim. The range was long for a handgun, but his bullet struck the animal just to the back of the eye, and its screams were instantly silenced. The horse fell, with Hollick, apparently lifeless, slumping forward but still in the saddle.

At that moment the shingles on the overburdened roof gave way, and a dozen or more men vanished from sight among shouts and screams and the rending of timber. Around the edges of the hole other men scrambled away, but the two boys hadn't moved. They remained frozen, their eyes apparently fixed on the rider who had finally come to rest, lying across the neck of the dead horse. The larger boy's features were hidden by a huge floppy-brimmed hat, but the younger one's eyes were wide and horror-stricken in a deathly white face.

Garvin took the quick route to the ground, sliding down the slope towards the heaving crowd at the rails of the corral. 'Move!' he yelled. A man below looked up just in time to skip clear before Garvin dropped off the edge. There were shouts of protest as his sudden descent brushed men aside, dealing out a few bruises on the way. Apparently oblivious, he landed with legs bent, going down into a roll which took him under the corral fence. The space around him was rapidly filling with men, some of them having jumped from the barn, others diving through the rails, eager to gawp at the dead stallion and the cowboy still draped across its neck. Many of them were arguing over the outcome of Hollick's ride; there had been a lot of money staked on him.

'Hollick's dead, all bets are off!' one man shouted.

'Hell, that ain't right,' a cowboy protested. 'Still in the saddle, ain't he?'

Thrusting the gamblers aside, a few strides took Garvin to the scene of carnage by the barn. More shingles were falling. The barn roof was creaking and the whole structure seemed ready to collapse, but still the boys clung to their unstable seat. Nobody seemed inclined to fetch them down.

Garvin leapt to stand on the black stallion's quarters. He reached up and grabbed the younger boy by the ankles, pulling hard, catching him as he fell, to half-toss him into the arms of one of the wranglers who'd held the stallion in the chute, a round-faced man who stared goggle-eyed at his burden. The older boy hadn't waited for Garvin to swing round again; as he faced back to the barn he saw the youngster already in mid-air. Cursing, caught off balance and with no clear idea where he'd end up,

Garvin made a grab as the youngster plunged head first towards the ground, his big hat wrapping itself over his face. Garvin managed to take hold of the back of the over-large shirt and jerk the boy right side up, slowing his descent.

They landed together, arms and legs entangled, each hindering the other's attempt to get to his feet. Coming upright at last the boy started to yell, his voice high and cracking with emotion. 'You're crazy! Just plain stupid. And look what's happened. You never took a minute to think. Of all the damnfool idiotic . . .' the words faded into sobs, the youngster's fists flailing, thumping into Garvin's ribs. He grabbed at the skinny wrists and held them. 'I just saved your neck, you ungrateful little—' He broke off, realizing the boy wasn't hearing him. The kid wasn't shouting at his rescuer, but at the man who lay sprawled over the dead horse.

The front of Hollick's skull had been cracked in two on impact with the barn. A little blood had trickled from his nose and mouth, and his eyes stared sightlessly at the dust. With a wail the youngster pulled free and flung himself on to the man's broken body.

'You'll be King Mo.' Garvin had worked his way around the crowd to reach the wagons and makeshift pens out back of the corral, searching for the man who had owned the stallion.

'And you're the bastard who shot my horse.' King Mo was a huge man, as tall as Garvin and twice as wide. His skin was as black as ebony. He was dressed in a fancy embroidered vest, and the hand that was inching towards the pearl-handled revolver tucked into his waistband sported several thick gold rings.

'You won't be needing that,' Garvin said, nodding towards the gun. Suddenly there was a .45 in his hand, its muzzle pointing steadily at King Mo's barrel-like chest. As the big Negro obediently froze, Garvin stepped up and dragged the revolver from its place. He was out of reach before the other man even thought of trying to stop him.

'That's better.' Garvin tossed the fancy gun behind him.

'What do you want?' The giant's lip curled. 'If you're after money then I'd advise you to think again. Robbing me would be a quick way to end up dead.'

'I just want you to answer me a question or two. What was the first name of that man who just died?'

The black man stared at him in disbelief. 'You holdin' me up because you want to know about some footloose cowboy?'

'His name,' Garvin persisted.

'Brad. His name was Brad Hollick.'

'Those two kids, are they his?'

'I guess so. Where he goes, they get underfoot,' King Mo replied. 'I got no reason to care, mister.'

'What about family?' When the big man didn't reply Garvin cocked the .45. 'I asked you a question. Did Hollick have any family? A brother, maybe?'

'How would I know? He was a cowboy, came to ride my horse.' King Mo glowered. 'The stallion that was making me good money until you put a bullet in its head.'

'I never saw a horse worth a cent once its legs were broke,' Garvin said, 'and if I hadn't stopped it I reckon there'd have been more than one man dead.'

The big man shrugged. 'Boot Hill ain't overcrowded. You'll want to bear that in mind if you're planning to rob me.'

'I told you, I'm not after your blood money. And your

wranglers are busy right now. Figure you'll want to calm things down some, before that mob get tired of fighting each other and start looking for you. Don't reckon you'll want them busting up your camp.' Beyond their small refuge the ruckus had reached ear-splitting proportions; the fights had become general, though as yet there was no gunplay.

'Seems to me Hollick rode that horse till it couldn't go any further,' Garvin said reasonably. 'You settle up now and you'll still have a business to run. All you have to do is pay what's due to him, and you'll quiet that mob down. I imagine the sheriff'll back you, seeing he had his money on Hollick.'

'I can't pay money to a dead man,' the giant said.

'No, but you can pay it to his sons,' Garvin said, 'they're right outside.'

King Mo laughed. 'An' if I don't? Are you going to shoot me? You won't even make it out of town.'

In answer, Garvin stepped in, fast and neat, the gun never wavering. His free hand took a grip of the black man's arm, while his foot stamped down on his instep. With a quick twist he threw King Mo to the ground, as if the giant weighed no more than the kid he had just dragged off the roof.

The big man landed face down, with Garvin kneeling on his back, the gun grinding into his arm just below the shoulder. 'If I pull this trigger,' he said softly, 'You maybe won't have anyplace to wear those fancy rings. You hear me? I got some powerful good reasons for wanting those kids to have that money. What do you say?'

'If I give them five hundred dollars how long do you think they'll keep it?' King Mo replied, trying to twist his head so he could see his captor. 'Some smart-ass will steal it before they get out of this one-horse town.'

'That's no concern of yours. They get the money, you keep those pretty rings on your fingers. Now, do we have a deal?'

'You'd better be a real fast mover,' King Mo growled. 'Sure, I'll pay up. But if you ain't out of town fast as lightning, you're dead.'

'If that's so, then you're coming to hell with me,' Garvin replied evenly. 'Was I you, I'd keep real quiet about what happened here; you don't want folks to know how easily King Mo got beat, do you?' As he spoke he stood up, holstering the .45. 'That's close to a riot going on out there. You got that five hundred bucks?'

King Mo nodded, glowering at Garvin as he brushed dust off his clothes.

'Fine. You go give it to those poor orphan boys. And don't think of setting your men on me, not if you need them to keep this outfit working.'

The sheriff stood swaying in the centre of the corral, his clothes dishevelled and his face bright red, a heaving mass of fighting men seething all around him. Seeing King Mo with Garvin he took a step towards them. A fist shot out from somewhere in the crowd and caught the sheriff on the side of his head.

With a roar the lawman flattened his assailant with a sideways swipe of his forearm, grabbing the man's revolver from his holster as he went down. With this in his hand he beat a clear path, stepping over a couple of bodies on the way before he stood breathing hard at King Mo's side. The lawman lifted his hand and fired off every round in the cylinder, then threw the empty gun aside.

'Listen up!' Before the sheriff could say a word King Mo's mighty voice echoed over the corral and the lull

27

brought about by the volley of shots became a silence. 'Brad Hollick won. I'm paying out.' He took a wad of bills from inside his vest and glanced around. The hatchet-faced wrangler stood nearby, blood dripping from a cut above one eye. 'Towse, go fetch me Hollick's kids,' King Mo barked. 'You hear, Sheriff? Guess you'll back me on this. Those who bet on Hollick have won.'

'Sure thing,' the sheriff agreed, a grin spreading across his face. 'Anybody wants to argue, they can cool their heels in my jail.'

The wrangler returned, dragging the struggling young-sters with him while a dishevelled crowd followed, pushing on his heels, eager to see what was happening.

'Here,' King Mo thrust the bundle of bills at the older boy, giving Garvin a malevolent sidelong glare. 'That's the purse I offered for anyone who could ride the black to a standstill. Your pa earned it.'

The older boy made no answer, staring down at the money in his hand, his face invisible beneath the wide floppy brim of his hat. It was the younger boy whose gaze ranged over King Mo's face, darting from him to the sher-iff and Garvin, then back to the big black man.

'Where are we supposed to go?' he asked. 'What are we gonna do?'

'That ain't my concern. You got money to pay for your pa's funeral, so get him out of my sight real quick, I got a business to run.' King Mo lifted a hand to the crowd, rais-ing his voice. 'One hour, folks, just time enough to go and wash the dust out of your throats. Then you get back here and I promise you a show.'

The covered wagon jolted over the ruts as it pulled out of Dobie's Bluff. Cole Garvin rode alongside, keeping an eye

28

on the few people who were out so early in the morning; he didn't think King Mo would follow up on his threats, but he'd be happier once he'd shaken loose of the rodeo. The older Hollick boy was at the reins, controlling the team with an ease that spoke of long practice. He shook the horses into a reluctant trot as if he too were eager to leave the town behind.

As their father was laid to rest the tall gangly youth had stood silent in his overlarge shirt, head down, not even removing the floppy-brimmed hat, and not speaking a word. It was the younger boy who went with Garvin to pay the undertaker from the stack of bills, as it had been the younger boy who led Garvin to their wagon, pointing out the horses that once belonged to their father, and that were now theirs.

'Mr Garvin, where are we going?' With Dobie's Bluff no more than a smear of dark smudges on the horizon behind them the younger boy stood up to look over his brother's head, only to be pulled back to the seat. He leant forward, peering around the hunched figure holding the reins. 'We going to your place, Mr Garvin? Is that what we're gonna do?'

'No. Not my place. We need to find somebody who can take care of you two. Before we left I talked to a few of the cowboys. I hear your pa had a brother. Is that right?'

'Sure. You saying we're gonna find Uncle Tom?'

'That's the idea.'

'It's a while since we saw him,' the boy replied, giving his brother a sidelong look. 'He's like Pa, don't care to settle much in one place.'

Garvin shrugged. He rode in silence for a while, staring straight ahead. 'You got a name, kid?' He asked at last.

'Sure. I'm Johnny. and this here's Al.'

29

'Al doesn't say much,' Garvin remarked, trying to see the face beneath that ever-present hat. If he hadn't seen and heard him yell the day before he might have thought the boy was dumb, or retarded. 'How about it, Al? You figure it's a good idea to look for your uncle? Maybe you know where to look?'

The only reply he got was a brief shake of the head. Garvin's mouth twisted into a humourless smile. He could be a patient man if need be, for a while.

CHAPTER FOUR

They came at nightfall. Three riders charged the solitary wagon, shooting into the air as their horses trampled through the campfire, hurling down the pot that hung over a meagre flame, and yelling Garvin's name. Nobody returned their fire. It took King Mo's wranglers a second to realize the campsite was deserted; two horses shifted uneasily under a solitary tree, rolling their eyes at the intruders.

'Hey, where'd he go?' One man lit down, throwing his reins to another. He grabbed a brand from the remains of the fire, blowing on it to resurrect a flame, and jumped on to the front of the wagon. Finding a lamp hanging on a hook he lit it, before throwing his makeshift torch on the ground. 'Nobody in here neither.'

'Garvin was with the kids when he left town. He can't be far away.'

'You ready to bet on that? His horse ain't here.' The third man's hatchet face was marked with a black eye and a swollen lip. He was circling uneasily, peering across the dark expanse of prairie. There was no shelter anywhere close, that was why they had ridden up fast, sure they could cut off Garvin's escape if he made a run for it. He reloaded

31

his six-gun before slipping it back into his holster. 'You figure he took the money, then left the kids?'

'Left 'em where?' The man on the wagon was throwing down blankets, a pair of tin plates, a coffee pot that hit the ground with a musical clang. He heaved a sack of grain to the back and tipped the contents out. A chest followed, bursting open to spill out clothes and a couple of books as its corner hit the ground.

The wrangler holding the horses was the round-faced man who had caught Johnny Hollick after Garvin pulled him from the roof. He dismounted, hitching the animals' reins around a rock. Having rooted through the garments he slammed the empty trunk shut. 'We could set light to this stuff,' he suggested. 'If they're hidin' someplace that'll fetch 'em.' He swivelled, scanning the camp. 'Maybe he killed 'em. Could be they're buried right under our feet.'

'What would he want to do that for? You ain't too hot when it comes to brains, Dan. If he killed 'em they'd still be here, the ground's hard as iron.' The rider went on circling the perimeter, peering into the near-dark. 'And don't go settin' light to nothin' in there, Whip, not unless you're damn sure King's money ain't hidden in that wagon.' He rode under the lone tree, where the horses had relaxed again, heads down, each resting a hoof. With a sudden jerk of the rein he brought his mount to a halt. 'Hey, Dan, bring a light here,' he ordered.

The man called Dan obeyed, stirring up the fire until the wood was burning fiercely, then grabbing the end of a thick branch and carrying it to the tree. Two pairs of eyes, betrayed by the flickering flame, stared down at him from the uppermost boughs.

Dan laughed. 'We should've guessed, Towse. Them's a pair of squirrels, lookit the way they hung on to that roof when their pa got hisself killed.'

With a nod the other man reined his horse back a few steps. 'You kids comin' down, or do we try some squirrel shootin'?'

'We're coming.' A small figure, bareheaded, lowered himself to the ground. 'Listen mister, we don't have that money. He took it.'

'So, Garvin ran out on you, huh?' Towse spat expressively into the dust. 'Figure we'll just make sure you ain't lyin' to us, boy. Search him, Dan.'

The wrangler obeyed. He found two bits in the boy's pocket. 'That's all he's got,' he said, showing it to Towse. 'If it's here the other one must have it.'

'Call your brother down, kid.' Towse ordered. 'We won't hurt you none if you're tellin' us the truth.'

'Come on, Al,' the boy said, as Dan released him. 'Ain't no good stayin' up there. Come down.'

'You heard your brother, Al,' Dan said, his round face split like a melon when he grinned. 'Quit playin' at bein' a squirrel an' get on down here.'

After a few seconds the second youngster, grotesque in floppy hat and baggy shirt, jumped to the dirt at their feet.

'Nothin' in the wagon.' The third man came to join them, tossing a battered book into the fire. 'If Garvin ain't taken it then they got it on 'em.'

'Hell, what you wearing that stupid thing for, kid. Bet you can't see me no better'n I can see you.' Towse leant down from the saddle and grabbed at the taller youngster's hat. The boy ducked aside, clutching at the wide brim, but the move came too late; Towse swept the hat off and threw it into the fire.

A tangle of bright chestnut hair fell around skinny shoulders. With a sideways glance at the men the youngster turned to run, heading fast into the darkness.

'That ain't no boy.' Towse spurred his horse and swooped down on the fugitive, leaping from the saddle and landing heavily on his prey, pinning the youngster in the dirt like a calf due for branding. After a long, charged moment the man got to his feet. Dragging the reluctant Al with him, he headed back to the fire, where the hat was burning brightly, adding new life to the flames as if in betrayal of the youngster, who stood with bowed head, silent and still.

His fingers digging into soft flesh, Towse turned the youngster's face, half-obscured by the thick wavy hair, so it was angled towards the firelight. A pair of angry grey eyes stared back at him, from a countenance that had nothing masculine about it.

'We-ell.' Dan laughed again. 'So that's what was hidin' under that hat.'

Towse stared at the girl, his eyes travelling down over the baggy shirt and pants she wore. 'Looks like Garvin's some kind of a fool, I bet he didn't know what he'd got right under his nose. Don't reckon he would've run out if he'd seen what I see.' He gave a mirthless laugh. 'You hiding something more than we can see under that shirt, missy? Maybe we'd better search you too, huh?'

'Garvin took the money,' Johnny said, his voice shrill. 'Tell them, Al.'

'It's true.' The girl's voice was steady. 'We don't have it. He rode out a couple of hours before sundown, and he told us not to try and follow him. If you get on the trail north you'll catch him.'

'No hurry. We've got time to check you out first.' Letting go of her chin, Towse seized the front of her shirt and pulled hard, nearly dragging her off her feet before the buttons gave way. The girl tried to fight him, her fists clenched, but he merely swatted them away, swung her around and pulled the remains of the garment over her head. The flames leapt high as he tossed it after the hat.

The girl wore a length of cloth wrapped tight around her breasts. Without it there was no way the baggy shirt could have kept her secret hidden.

'Get that thing off,' Towse demanded, his voice suddenly husky.

'Hey, Towse, we're here to get the money,' Dan said uneasily, his round face creasing in concern. 'She's just a kid.'

'She's no kid,' Towse said, his gaze still on the girl. 'Kids don't have what she's got. We been put to a whole lot of trouble, an' we're owed somethin'. If we find the money it goes to King Mo, anythin' else I find is all mine. I'm gonna have me a good time. If you don't like it then ride on out of here.'

'Leave her be!' They had forgotten the boy, who flung himself at Towse, pummelling the man's ribs with futile blows. 'Leave her alone!'

'It's OK, kid,' Dan grabbed him, lifting him away as Towse's hand went to the gun on his hip. 'He ain't gonna do her no harm.'

'No,' Whip said, licking his lips as he moved closer, an evil grin on his face. 'Just gonna have us a bit of fun. See, we're gonna play a game or two, the sort the ladies like. She'll have a real nice time.'

'Get the kid out of here, Dan,' Towse ordered, 'then make up your mind. You want a piece of this tasty little sugar, it's yours for the takin'. If you don't then hit the trail.'

Dan hesitated a second then dragged the boy to the

wagon, avoiding the kicks Johnny aimed at his ankles. 'Quit that.' Dan picked him up and threw him bodily inside, on to the ruin of the children's possessions.

'Tell them to leave Al alone!' the boy demanded, scrambling back towards the wrangler, his fists clenched.

'Look, kid, you stir from here an' Towse's likely to forget you ain't a squirrel after all,' Dan warned. 'Ain't worth gettin' yourself shot for. If'n your sister behaves herself she won't get hurt too bad, it's somethin' that's gonna happen one o' these days, even sooner now you ain't got your pa takin' care of you. Might just as well be now. Sit quiet and you can both go on your way an' forget all about it come the mornin'.'

By way of answer the boy dived into the things littering the wagon. He came back up holding a frypan, swinging it at the wrangler's head.

'Dammit, didn't I tell you to quit?' Dan dodged the blow and dealt the boy an open-handed swipe that knocked the pan from his hands. He picked up a man's belt from the ruins strewn around them and dragged the boy's arms around behind his back. A shirt served to bind his legs. 'Now hush up. We'll be gone in a while.'

The man they called Whip was stirring up the fire, feeding it with things he'd thrown out of the wagon, tossing clothes and blankets into the flames until the campsite was brightly lit. 'C'mon, let's see what we got,' he urged, his hands busy at the front of his pants. 'Fair shares, Towse, you get to go first, but just 'cause you found her don't make her all yours.'

'Sure, I ain't arguin'. Reckon we gotta get this off fer ourselves, seeing she ain't willin'.' Towse said, giving up his attempt to strip the cloth from the girl's breasts. He pulled out a knife and took a grip on the top of the binding, his breath coming fast and noisy as her pale flesh caught the red light from the flames. 'Hold still,' he ordered, as his victim shrank away from his touch. He pressed the blade against the taut cloth.

Please.' The girl begged, half-lifting her hands as if to fend him off. 'Don't.'

Whip sniggered. 'Hell, missy, you better change your tune. What we got planned won't do you no harm, it's real nat'ral, like somethin' out o' the Bible. It'll be just like Adam an' Eve. Go ahead, Towse, slice it up, then I'll help you get them pants off her.'

The rip of cloth sounded loud over the crackle of the fire. Trying to hide her nakedness the girl pulled away from her tormentors. She stumbled and fell, landing at Whip's feet, her hair dangerously close to the fire. Whimpering, she rolled away from the heat and got to her knees, hands clasped to the pale swell of her breasts.

Towse slid his knife into its sheath, grabbed her by the ankle, and pulled her back to the ground. 'Come on, ain't no need to fight. We'll take real good care of you. You're gonna like it, you see if you don't.' She kicked out at him wildly, sobbing as much in fury as in fear.

Whip laughed, capering around as he tried to get a grip on the girl's legs. 'Reckon we'll have to hogtie this one. Maybe I'd best go fetch us a rope.'

A gunshot cracked, the sound sharp and clear in the cool air, and Towse flinched. He put one hand to the side of his head, where the top of his ear was spraying blood. The other dropped to his holster, coming up fast with a pistol in its grip. Even as he looked for the source of the shot, another slug spat through the night.

The expression on Towse's face changed from anger to faint surprise, then he folded forward and silently crumpled to the floor. Whip was turning, ducking, his gun spitting lead as he ran. From out of the darkness a third shot sounded. The slug took Whip high in the chest. He yelped, the gun slipping from his fingers as he dropped to his knees, all thought of resistance forgotten.

'Don't shoot!' Dan stepped away from the wagon, lifting his hands high above his head. He stared blindly into the gloom. 'Please. I didn't do nothin', I swear.'

There was the metallic sound of a gun being cocked. 'Please,' Dan said again, sweat breaking out on his face. 'I ain't gonna try nothin'.' Long moments passed, the silence total except for the crackle of the fire and the harsh moans from Whip's throat. Close to the injured man, the girl lay curled into a ball, as if that would hide her from their sight.

'Unbuckle your gun belt,' a harsh voice said at last. 'Left hand.'

Dan did as he was told, clumsy in his haste to obey. When the holstered gun thudded to the ground he stepped quickly away from it, stretching his arms for the stars again.

Cole Garvin strode into the circle of firelight. As he stared down at the girl he was paler than she, his face the colour of grey ash, and looking as if it had been carved from a block of granite. She glanced up through a veil of hair, giving him one brief horrified look before she scrambled to her feet, her hands wrapped tight across her chest, to flee into the darkness.

CHAPTER FIVE

Whip sat on the ground, blood oozing from between his fingers as he pressed his hand over the wound below his shoulder. Garvin reached down to pick up the gun the man had dropped. 'You want to give me one good reason why I shouldn't finish you?' he said, his voice cold as an arctic wind.

'She didn't come to no harm. An' I didn't touch her,' the man whined. 'I swear I didn't mean nothin'. It was Towse—'

Garvin slashed at the wrangler's face with the barrel of his own gun. 'That's a lie. I'm not blind and I'm not deaf. Try again, mister.'

'We was only gonna have us some fun.' Whip spoke with difficulty; his nose was broken and his top lip was split, the gore from his face running to mix with the blood still seeping from the bullet wound.

'I don't think she saw it that way.' Garvin's hand drew back for another blow.

'Please, mister.' The plea came from Dan. The wrangler was still straining his hands towards the stars, as he stood staring at Towse's dead body which lay on the ground between them. 'Whip was willin', ain't no denyin' that, but it was Towse who started it. I don't reckon you're the kind of fella who'd kill an unarmed man. Don't you reckon Whip's taken enough?'

Garvin said nothing, hard lines etched on his face, his eyes unyielding as flint.

'We was wrong.' Dan went on. 'Sure, we was wrong. But, hell, seein' her like that, it was so temptin'. A man can't help bein' the way he's made, can he, mister? Ain't easy when you see a woman half-naked right under your eyes, when you thought you was lookin' at a dumb kid.'

Garvin stared at him, spinning round suddenly when he heard a sound, the .45 at the ready, but it was only the girl. Another overlarge shirt shrouded her figure, and she'd found a bandanna to tie around her hair. Released from his bonds, Johnny came behind her, rubbing at his arms.

'Please, Mr Garvin, there's no need to hurt him any more.' Her voice was pitched low for a girl, yet there was something unmistakably feminine about it. Garvin understood why she had refused to talk to him before, a few words would have betrayed her. 'I'm all right.'

'You asking me to let them go?' he grated. 'Knowing what they would have done if I hadn't come back in time?'

'I can't say I'm sorry about . . .' she faltered, flashing a glance at Towse's body, 'but I don't want anybody else to die because of me.'

'We'll clear out,' Dan offered swiftly. 'I swear, you'll never see us again. I'm sorry we scared you, missy. Real sorry.'

For a long moment Garvin stood as if lost in thought, then he nodded. 'If I let you go, you tell King Mo to leave us be. If that black bastard sends anyone else after me, he'll be the one I come looking for. And tell him he'll never get his hands on that five hundred bucks. All but a few dollars spending money went into the bank for safe keeping before we left Dobie's Bluff.'

'Don't reckon I want to be the one to give King Mo no bad news. I'll be movin' on,' Dan said. 'But first I'll see Whip gets back to town, an' he can take your message.'

'Sure,' Whip said, exploring his bloody mouth with his tongue, 'I ain't plannin' to tangle with you again, mister. The King's leavin' Dobie's Bluff in a couple days, don't reckon he'll be comin' this way no more. He's heading for the easy money back East.'

With Garvin watching him, Dan buried Towse in a shallow grave, then did his best to tend Whip's wound. 'Now you ride,' Garvin said implacably. 'Come back and you're dead men.'

When the two riders had gone, Towse's horse trailing behind them, Garvin vanished into the darkness, returning a couple of minutes later leading his own mount. He threw a couple of jackrabbits at Johnny's feet. 'You know what to do with those?' he asked.

'Sure.' The boy nodded.

'Then get 'em cooking.' Garvin lifted to the saddle. 'I'll go make sure those two don't have second thoughts.'

Johnny harnessed the team as the sun rose off the horizon, chattering to Garvin who worked silently at his side.

'We was real glad you came back and got rid of those men last night, Mr Garvin,' the boy said. 'When you rode off before we'd set up camp, Al thought maybe you was leaving.'

'That meat I brought in beat the hard tack from the store, didn't it?' Garvin replied.

'Sure. Will you take me hunting some time? I can shoot

41

pretty good. Al's got that money; she won't tell me where it is, only that it's safe. Soon as we get to a town I can buy me a gun. Pa let me use his .22 until he had to sell it. We ran out of money. That's why he rode that stallion. Al didn't want him to. She said we could manage.'

Garvin nodded, making no reply.

'You ain't cross with Al, are you Mr Garvin?' Johnny asked suddenly. 'What happened yesterday wasn't her fault.'

'Her name can't be Al,' Garvin said.

Johnny grinned. 'Sure it is. She's Alicia really, but I've always called her Al, even when she was a girl. See, she used to wear skirts most of the time, but Pa started making her wear pants a couple of years back. I thought it was stupid, she's not much like a boy, except she can ride pretty good, but men got some strange ideas, don't they? Pa must've known I guess. He was pretty clever mostly, our pa.' He was quiet for a few seconds. 'Was that man right, Mr Garvin?'

'About what?'

'Not being able to help it. Being so mean to women-folk.' The boy stared up at him and Garvin looked away, his face turned back to stone.

'No, Johnny, don't reckon he was. You'll understand when you grow up some more. Sure, we've all got a bit of animal inside us, and sometimes we have to work to keep it under control. Reckon Dan meant there's times when maybe it's harder than others.'

The girl appeared on the wagon's seat, silently taking the reins as Johnny handed them up to her. She had replaced her hat with one that had been flung from the wagon the night before; it had escaped the fire but the brim was a little bent in places. It hid her hair but not her face; wearing that, nobody who got close was going to mistake her for a boy. As on the previous day, she didn't speak to Garvin as they took to the trail.

'Where are we going, Mr Garvin?' Johnny asked.

'Unless you know where we can find that uncle of yours, I was thinking of heading for a place along the Tamara River. It's either that or we go looking for the Circle S ranch. That name mean anything to you?'

'Never heard of it,' Johnny said, glancing at his sister who was ignoring them both. 'Who does it belong to?'

'Used to belong to a man called Willard Simons, but he's dead. Guess you don't recall hearing his name either?' He turned to the girl. 'I got places to go, quite a few of them. The pair of you are welcome to tag along, unless you got other plans. Sometime we have to track down your uncle. You maybe got some ideas about how we do that?'

She shook her head, not meeting his eyes, staring intently down at the horses.

'Then we're heading north, to the Tamara.'

He led them on to the trail, the ruins of many of the youngsters' belongings left among the ashes of the fire and scattered on the ground, while a low mound marked the last resting place of a man none of them would mourn. Scavengers and the ever-present wind would soon strip the place bare, and like many men before him, Towse would vanish into the dust.

It was slow travelling with the wagon, and Garvin considered leaving the two youngsters and riding on alone, but the memory of the scene by the campfire haunted him. Alicia Hollick bore no resemblance to his dead sister, yet in that instant when he'd returned to confront Towse and

43

Whip he'd known again the fury and anguish that possessed him when he saw Julie's defiled body.

He had come here seeking vengeance, driving himself hard so he didn't have to think, pushing his body to exhaustion then falling into a dreamless sleep when he eventually let himself rest. Intent only on his self-imposed task, he had taken up with the Hollick kids to find their uncle, and he would have deserted Johnny and Al without a qualm. Trouble was, Al had turned into Alicia, and everything had changed. He couldn't deny the girl was likely to take any man's eye, although, unlike the three wranglers, he had his appetites under control. If only she hadn't been so much in need of his protection; he felt torn, unwilling to desert her.

They stopped around noon. Johnny took the horses down to the river while Alicia busied herself in the wagon, blushing a little as she came to where Garvin hunkered by the newly lit fire. 'I want to say thank you,' she said, her voice pitched low so her brother wouldn't hear. 'If you hadn't stopped those men, they . . .' she broke off, the colour in her cheeks mounting. 'My father made me wear those things, to keep me safe. He was always saying he'd ride one more season and then we'd settle someplace, but somehow it never happened.'

'Man has to do what he's good at,' Garvin replied, keeping his eyes fixed on the flames he was tending. 'Seems to me you must have some family, someplace you and Johnny could go?'

She shook her head. 'No. There's only our uncle. And I reckon he's too much like Pa to be much use to us.'

'How old are you?' he asked abruptly.

'I don't know exactly. I was born in July, but I don't know what day. Come August I guess I can say I'm seventeen.'

Garvin didn't reply, but rose swiftly to his feet. 'We'll need more wood,' he said, turning his back to her and hurrying away. Julie had been seventeen when he'd left her with their aunt. For two long years he'd ignored her pleas to be allowed to join him, but eventually he'd given in. He would never forgive himself for not leaving her where she was safe.

From then on Garvin rode ahead, staying away from the youngsters except when they camped for the night, and even then finding excuses not to be close to the girl. Still there were times when he couldn't help noticing the way the light caught Alicia's bright hair, and that she had a way of smiling that emphasized the fullness of her lips. The curves of her body, no longer disguised but showing plain under the man's shirt she had taken to wearing again, filled his head with feelings he didn't want to acknowledge.

She rarely spoke to him, but sometimes when she was talking to Johnny the sound of her voice would bring an unwelcome warmth to his body. He would turn away, cursing himself, and wincing if he heard her laugh. He was no longer sleeping sound at night. Staring up at the stars he would tell himself she was a child, the same age as Julie had been when last he'd seen her, two years before her death.

It was a relief when they came at last to the bend in the Tamara river, where a ramshackle cabin leant drunkenly against a cluster of rocks and a chattering stream came down from the hills to meet the main flow a few yards from the ruin. This was the place the sheriff of Dobie's Bluff had described to him, the place where Josiah Marriday had once panned for gold.

After telling Johnny to pull the wagon under the trees

and ignoring the enquiring look the girl gave him, Garvin rode on alone, but he already knew what he would find. There was a hole in the cabin's roof, and when he pushed the sagging door open to look inside, he could see nobody had lived there for years.

Garvin gave the crumbling timber a hefty kick and part of the wall fell with a muted crash, exploding in a cloud of dust.

'I could just see Pa doing that exact same thing. Guess all men think with their muscles instead of their heads.' The girl had followed him in silence, and the sound of her voice made him whip round to face her. Her lips were curved into a half-smile; at that moment Alicia Hollick had nothing of the child about her. 'What good was that supposed to do?'

'That's no business of yours,' Garvin said angrily.

'Isn't it?' She gave him a level stare, the smile vanishing. 'You didn't make King Mo give us that money because you felt sorry for a couple of orphans. And if you wanted to steal it you've had plenty of chances, so how come I've still got it? The last two days you've been like a bear with a sore head, just itching to ride on and leave us. I can't figure out why you're still here, Mr Garvin. Come to that I don't know why we're here either. I think it's time you told us.'

CHAPTER SIX

Garvin gave the girl a long hard look, wondering what to tell her. Fact was, he didn't have much of an answer. He had to track down the youngsters' uncle, but if he told them he thought the man might be a killer they'd clam up for good. Since he'd set out to seek justice for his sister he'd laid aside his conscience; he'd used force a time or two when folks didn't want to talk to him, but faced with Alicia and Johnny Hollick he was well and truly stymied.

'What do you want with us?' Alicia persisted.

'Leave him be, Al.' Johnny came at a run, his young face creased into a frown. 'He's our friend, ain't right to go pushin' him. You sure didn't mind when he drove off them wranglers.'

The girl flushed. 'I thanked him for that. There was no need for him to stay once they'd gone.'

'That's stupid, an' you know it.' The kid was really getting his dander up, his voice rising. 'You think you're real grown up, but we ain't gonna last long on our own. How long before we meet up with more men like that?'

Garvin put a hand on the boy's shoulder. 'It's OK, Johnny, your sister's got a point. I reckon right now we'd all feel better with a cup of coffee inside us. Why don't you finish seeing to the team and I'll get a fire started. We'll sit and talk this over.'

'I don't care why you're here. Ain't no business of mine.' The boy pulled a face at his sister and turned his back on them. Once he'd tended the horses he kept his distance, going off to poke about in the ruined cabin, ignoring Alicia when she called to tell him the coffee was hot.

'Leave him be,' Garvin said, as he sat down opposite the girl. 'He's kind of young to be hearing what I have to say.' Keeping his gaze on the fire, he told the story in as few words as possible, starting with the day he went to Sykes' Pass to meet his sister, and leaving out nothing but his suspicions about the involvement of Tom Hollick. When he'd finished there was silence.

'How old was she?' Alicia said at last. Her voice was so soft he could barely make it out.

'Just a kid, a couple of years older than you.'

'I'm not a kid,' she said, her chin coming up. 'Johnny's a kid.' She glanced at the edge of the river. Her brother had found some old tools and he stood in the shallows searching for gold, enthusiastically swilling water around a rusty old pan.

'Have it your own way,' Garvin said. 'You got your answer. I helped you out in Dobie's Bluff because I figured you needed it, but I'm still around because I need to talk to your uncle. He was on that stage, same as the old man who used to live here.'

'You can't really think Uncle Tom knows anything about that gang,' Alicia said angrily, her eyes flashing fire. 'He's not a thief, and he's not a murderer. I know he wouldn't do what those men did. He's like Pa, he'll maybe break the law sometimes, but he wouldn't hurt anybody.'

'Once we track him down he can tell me that for himself,' Garvin replied reasonably.

'Maybe he's dead. Maybe the men who robbed the stage killed him.'

'Me and the marshal would've found him.' Garvin pushed to his feet. 'If you won't help me I'll still find him; makes no difference. I'll find Marriday first if I can, at least I've got some kind of lead on where he might be. Fact is, I can't see an old soak like him getting caught up with a gang of thieving murderers. They wouldn't have been able to trust him to keep quiet. On the other hand, I gather your uncle was generally broke, and you said yourself he's been known to break the law.'

The girl's mouth was set in an obstinate line. 'I hope you never find either of them. The old man hasn't been here anyway, and you don't know where else to look.'

'I don't reckon he'll be far from the nearest saloon, and seeing he wasn't around Dobie's Bluff that probably means he ended up at Sykes' Pass. Always was a long shot, coming out here.' He scowled at the cabin. 'Don't see how the sheriff could have got it so wrong. Must be ten years since that place was fit to live in.'

The girl came to stand at his side. 'What will you do to him?' she demanded, and he knew she wasn't referring to Marriday.

He swung back. 'Make him tell me the truth,' he said. 'If you're right about the sort of man Tom Hollick is then he's got nothing to fear from me, but I swore I'd kill the men who took Julie's life. If he's one of them, him being your uncle makes no difference.'

'He's been seen right here in town and you haven't talked to him?' Garvin stared down at Marshal Tate, his face hard.

49

'I've been busy. Only got back yesterday.' Tate replied mildly, leaning back in his swivel chair until it groaned in protest. 'You saying I ain't doing my job?'

Garvin shook his head. 'No. Sorry, Mike, guess I'm out of line. So, where am I likely to find Josiah Marriday now?'

'He'll be in one of the cheap joints on the edge of town,' Tate replied. With a sigh he rose slowly to his feet. 'I got my job to do, Cole. Until they vote me out I'm the law around here. Reckon I have to be there when you talk to any man who was on that stage.'

'I'm not looking to cause trouble,' Garvin said. 'All I want is answers.'

Tate's eyebrows shot up. 'You expect me to believe that? I was there that day, remember?' He swept his hat on to his head. 'C'mon, with a bit of luck old Maddy's not had time to drink himself under the table yet.'

'You root out any more about the other passenger?' Garvin asked, as he followed Tate from his office.

'Hollick? No. But I can tell you why they chose to hold up that stage. Turns out Will Simons was carrying a lot of money. And I mean a lot. Figured on doing a deal for a piece of land, and the man who was selling it didn't trust banks. Along with what was in the mail they got away with quite a haul.'

Garvin was silent a while, thinking about Julie, and the simple bad luck that had put her on that particular stage-coach.

'Last I heard you reckoned you were close to finding Hollick yourself,' Tate said, rousing him from his reverie.

'I found his brother,' Garvin replied, 'only he died before I had a chance to talk to him. Got himself killed by a crazy mustang, all for the sake of a few hundred bucks.' He told Tate about the rodeo, and what he'd been doing since he left Dobie's Bluff.

'So where are these two kids of his?' Tate asked, looking mystified.

'A few hours behind me, I guess. They want to stop me finding their uncle. And since they don't have no place else to go, they're clinging to me worse than a couple of burrs.'

'You call them kids, but by the sound of it the girl is near enough grown up.' Tate said. 'Could be they'll get themselves into a heap of trouble driving around the prairie on their lonesome.'

'You telling me I owe them something?'

'Maybe you will, pretty soon,' Tate told him. 'Even if their uncle's a murderer, he's all they've got. Be hard on them if he ends up dead.'

They found the man they were looking for in a tumble-down place called Heafy's. Josiah Marriday sat alone at the bar's solitary table, staring gloomily into an empty glass. His thin hair was dirty grey, straggling down on to the collar of his filthy shirt. He turned bleary eyes on the marshal. 'You buyin'?' he asked hopefully.

'Maybe later,' Tate replied, taking the old man by the arm and pulling him outside. 'We'll find us a nice quiet place to have a chinwag. And you,' he added, pointing a stubby finger at Garvin, 'keep your mouth shut until I say different.'

'All right, Maddy,' Tate said, once they were hunkered down in the shade. 'Tell me how come you were on the stage out of Indian Flats a couple of months back.'

The old man licked dry lips, giving Garvin a wary side-long look. 'I got me a ticket, Marshal. Wasn't doin' nothin' wrong.'

'How d'you get the fare?'

'Didn't say I paid for the ticket myself,' Marriday said. 'There was a fella owed me a favour. He was plannin' to take the stage but somethin' come up. Guess he knew I wanted to get out of town.'

'And why was that?'

The old man shrugged. 'There was a ruckus in the saloon. Wasn't my fault, but the sheriff said he'd lock me up an' throw away the key if I didn't get my hide out o' there.'

Tate snorted. 'Without the booze you'd be out of your mind in a week, and driving him crazy too. All right, Maddy, so you got a ticket for the stage. How come you weren't on it when it got robbed?'

'Who says I wasn't?'

At that Garvin leant across and grabbed the old man's collar. 'They killed four people,' he ground out. 'You saying they left a useless old piece of shit like you alive?'

'That's enough!' Tate fastened his hand around Garvin's wrist, gripping hard until the other man released his hold. 'Let him finish.'

With a wordless growl Garvin backed off.

'You know any of those folks on the stage, Maddy?' Tate asked.

Marriday edged away from Garvin before he replied, watching him through wary, bloodshot eyes. 'Sure. I never met the drummer before, but he was pretty generous with the bottle he was carryin'. After two days we was real friendly.'

'Anyone else?'

'Bert Calloway was drivin'. An' there was Mr Simons from the Circle S. His pappy was a friend of mine. Mr Simons don't mind buyin' a man a drink when he's down on his luck.'

Garvin gave an angry snort and Marriday flinched, though seeing Tate give the other man a warning look he seemed to take courage. 'How come you're so interested, mister?' he asked. 'You work for Wells Fargo?'

'No.' Garvin said shortly.

'No,' Marriday repeated, his eyes widening a little as he fixed his gaze on Garvin. 'The girl. Ain't much of a likeness, her bein' real purty an' all, but you got the same eyes. Same mouth, too.'

'She was my sister. And she's dead. We know you were on the stage when it left the way station. How come you're still alive?' Garvin demanded harshly.

The old man's gaze flickered uneasily between the two men. 'Mr Simons,' he said at last, 'he knew somethin' was goin' on. That mornin' he got a good look at the fella ridin' shotgun. He said we was in for trouble. An' he said somethin' about makin' a mistake, trustin' a man just because he wore a badge.'

'What?' It was Tate who grabbed hold of Marriday this time. 'Who was he talking about?'

'He didn't say.' The drunkard shrunk from him. 'Guess he might've done, only once he told me there was likely gonna be a hold-up, I didn't figure to hang around an' find out. I got a powerful dislike of gettin' shot.'

'This isn't making sense.' Garvin said harshly. 'You couldn't have escaped. The shotgun was in on the robbery, he wouldn't have let the driver set you down. If you weren't in on it, they wouldn't have let you get away.'

'The stage didn't stop,' Marriday said. 'When it slowed down to cross Half-hide Creek, I opened the door an' jumped. Water was low.'

'You jumped?' Garvin was incredulous. 'How come you didn't break your damn neck?'

'Reckon I can answer that,' Tate put in. 'He stole a bottle at the way station the night before. What with that and the drummer's whiskey I doubt if he even felt it when he hit the water.'

'Then he should have drowned,' Garvin snarled angrily.

The sun was going down. Sykes' Pass came back to life as the heat of the day faded. Cole Garvin brushed crumbs off his vest as he strode out of the cheap eating joint, angling across the street towards the livery stable. Marriday had given him no leads on Tom Hollick. The old drunkard had no interest in a drifter with empty pockets, but he'd said he would recognize the member of the gang who'd ridden shotgun, the elusive Zeke Dailey. That might prove useful, if only he knew where to look for the man.

Garvin had no clear idea of where he would go next, but he was eager to move on; he wouldn't find Hollick by hanging around town. Young Johnny had told him his uncle used to turn up at the rodeo now and then. Since he had no better ideas he would go back to King Mo's outfit and start again from there. As he led his mount from the stables, a two-horse rig came into sight, the driver silhouetted against the lowering sun. The light formed a halo around the girl's tangle of bright hair, which she had let loose to cascade to her shoulders.

Alicia whipped up the reluctant horses and they surged into a fast trot as she headed straight for Garvin. 'Well?' she demanded, reining in the team. 'Did you find the man you were looking for?'

'I found him. Now I'm moving on.' He turned his back on her to put his foot in the stirrup, only to find she had thrown the reins to her brother and leapt to the ground, coming to grab hold of his arm.

'Leave him alone,' she begged. 'Please. He didn't do it, I swear he didn't.'

He pulled free and lifted into the saddle, neck-reining the horse to side-step around her. 'If that's so he's got nothing to be afraid of,' Garvin said.

'Garvin!' Marshall Tate came running down the street. 'Hold on.'

'What's up, Mike?' Garvin asked, turning to face him.

'You saying you don't know?' the lawman's face was hard. Suddenly there was a Colt repeater in his hand, coming up fast as he drew a bead on Garvin's chest. 'Step out of the saddle, and keep your hands where I can see 'em.'

'You're making a mistake, Marshal, I've done nothing wrong.'

'I wish I could believe you.' Tate tossed a coin to Johnny Hollick. 'When you've seen to your team, kid, take that horse back into the livery. It won't be needed tonight. Unbuckle your gunbelt, Garvin, and let it drop. You're under arrest.'

CHAPTER SEVEN

'Where are we going?' Garvin asked, as Marshall Tate motioned him to cross the street in front of him.

'Reckon you know the way to Heafy's bar by now,' Tate ground out. 'We'll step around the back, there's something I want you to see. And make it fast, the light's going.'

Behind Heafy's bar long shadows lay across the waste ground that ran down to a pool of stagnant water. Garvin hesitated.

'Straight ahead.' Tate gestured with the Colt. Obediently Garvin picked a path through the mess of empty bottles and other trash in his way, coming to a stop at the muddy edge of the water hole. Something lay in the shallows, half in and half out of the pool. It looked like a bundle of old rags, except for the pale shape that clutched at the mud with crooked fingers. Garvin bent closer. In the very last of the daylight he could make out Maddy Marriday's head, the sparse hair clinging to the old man's skull, the bloodshot eyes staring sightlessly at him from beneath an inch of water.

'What happened?' Garvin asked, spinning round to face the marshal. 'You don't think I had anything to do with this? He must've got a skinful once too often, lost his way when he came out of the bar.'

'Pull him out,' Tate said harshly.

With a shrug Garvin did as he was bid, taking hold of the arm that lay out of the water. The mud gave up its burden with an obscene sucking sound.

'We'll need a light. Best bring him to the street,' Tate ordered. 'Just so you can take a real good look.'

When the body lay outside Heafy's sagging door, Tate reached to lift down the lamp that hung at the entrance and rubbed at the sooty glass with his sleeve, then thrust the lantern down so it was inches from the dead face. 'You see plain enough now?' he demanded. 'You still telling me you don't know nothing about this? Seem to recall you saying the man should've died in the river.'

Josiah Marriday's scrawny neck was splotched with dark marks, and his tongue protruded from between his lips.

'A man don't look like that when he drowns,' Tate went on coldly. 'And you're the only one with a reason to kill him.'

'What reason?' Garvin rounded on him angrily. 'I never thought he was in cahoots with the gang.'

'Maybe not, but he was there on that stage, and he ran out when there was trouble. Could be you figure if he'd stayed it might have played out different, especially if Simons tried to make a fight of it.'

'Do I really look that stupid? What use would this drunken old coward have been? I set out to find the men who killed my sister, Tate. Marriday wasn't one of them. And if you're looking for a reason for him getting killed, could be he gave it to us a few hours back. He had a good look at the man who was riding shotgun that day, and he said he'd know him again for sure. Maybe you've forgotten; there wasn't a soul in Indian Flats who was willing to say the same.'

'Real convenient,' Tate growled, 'somebody coming

along to kill him right after you came to town.'

'Seems to me the gang who held up the stage would find it mighty convenient if I got locked up in jail for something I didn't do,' Garvin shot back. 'Marriday told us there was a lawman involved in the hold-up. Maybe Simons was talking about you.'

Tate sucked in a breath and rocked back on his heels, the Colt swinging up in his hand as if he meant to bring the butt down on Garvin's head. Seeing his one chance of escape, though knowing it was a slim one, Garvin didn't wait for the blow to fall but dived in beneath it while the lawman had given up his chance of loosing off a shot.

Garvin's two fists ploughed into Tate's belly and the gun flew from the lawman's hand. He was sent reeling backwards, saved from falling only by the wall of Heafy's bar. The whole building shook under Tate's weight, but he came bouncing back, his hands clenching into fists. Garvin didn't give the marshal time to get a single punch in, landing a fiery uppercut on Tate's jaw that snapped his head around to thud into the wooden wall again. The lawman staggered, and Garvin's fingers closed around the gun he'd dropped, tossing it towards the distant pool where they'd found Marriday's body. Before Tate could recover, Garvin grabbed him by one arm, spun him around and threw him flat on his face. He followed him down, to land kneeling on the lawman's back, keeping his grip on the man's arm and twisting it high. A low moan issued from Tate's lips.

Garvin eased back a little. 'Was it you?' he demanded. 'You knew Simon, were you the one he shouldn't have trusted?'

'No!' The marshal struggled, trying to throw Garvin off, 'are you crazy? You ain't helping yourself, Garvin. Was this how it was with Maddy? Were you trying to make him talk?'

'I never touched him.' Garvin hesitated. Every instinct told him Tate wasn't the man who betrayed Simons, but the marshal was set on blaming him for Marriday's death, and he didn't have time to convince him otherwise. 'I'm sorry, Mike,' he said, bringing his left fist across and hitting the other man hard behind his ear. The lawman collapsed to the ground without a sound.

Garvin put his head down and listened, relieved to hear deep regular breathing. He picked the marshal up and carried him round behind the bar, where he used the man's bandanna and belt to tie his hands and feet.

Back at the livery yard Johnny Hollick was still busy with the wagon team, which meant Garvin's horse was hitched to the rail, saddled and bridled and ready to run. Garvin dragged the rein free just as Alicia came from the back of the wagon.

'What are you doing?' She ran to block his path.

'Leaving,' he said. 'Where I go is no business of yours.'

'It is when you're trying to kill the only family we've got left,' she cried, leaping forward and making a grab at his rein. 'Please.' She half-turned her head. 'Johnny, get the horses hitched up again. Quick.'

'You planning to follow me?' Garvin stopped trying to pull the rein from her hands, suddenly weary.

'I'll do whatever I can to stop you hurting Uncle Tom,' she said passionately.

'If you're so sure he's innocent then help me find him,' Garvin suggested.

'Mr Garvin?' The light of dawn showed Johnny Hollick's face pale and drawn, his eyes red from lack of sleep, but he held the reins firm as the team scented water and tried to increase their speed. 'We gonna stop soon?'

'Sure. We'll let the horses drink, then drive downstream a while. Water's real shallow right now.'

'You think the marshal's comin' after us?'

'I don't know, but if he is we've given him plenty to think about. Don't reckon he'll untangle our trail too easy.' Garvin waited impatiently while the animals drank their fill. 'Keep them steady now,' he warned. 'Don't want them getting colic. We'll let them rest as soon as we're well out of sight.'

'Are you really gonna let us stay with you?'

'Will you quit asking that?' Garvin said irritably. 'I said you could, didn't I?'

'But you said we couldn't come all the way,' Johnny replied.

'We're heading for Dobie's Bluff. All I said was, I need to go and check it out first. If King Mo's moved on then it'll be safe for you and your sister to go into town. Quit pestering me, kid.'

The boy returned his look, his jaw set. 'Al says you don't really want us along. She says you'll dump us again, soon as you get the chance.'

Garvin sighed. 'Is that so?'

Johnny wasn't ready to give up. He glanced at the hunched figure behind him, well wrapped in blankets and apparently sound asleep. 'She woke up a while back. She said she bet you were already wishing you could get rid of us.'

'Well, I guess your clever sister knows everything, like most women, so maybe she's got that right. Look kid, you and Alicia can do whatever you want, come or stay, it's no skin off my nose. Hell, I got you that money didn't I? Find yourself a room someplace.'

The boy stared at him for a few seconds, then shook his

head 'No siree. Al says if you find Uncle Tom we gotta be there.'

Garvin glared at the boy, not knowing whether to laugh or curse. Before he could make up his mind the girl stirred beneath the blankets.

'Pull up under those trees, we'll stop here,' Garvin said shortly, turning to spur his horse away before Alicia Hollick was awake enough to start her own attack on him. Between the two of them, the youngsters could get under his skin faster than a tree full of bees.

He kept his distance, only joining them for a few minutes once Johnny summoned him to breakfast, and making his escape before they finished eating, busying himself with the horses, taking each of them to the river in turn and washing the sweat from their hides.

'You can't avoid us for ever.'

Garvin's head jerked up. Alicia Hollick stood on the bank, a mug of coffee in each hand. 'Can't we have a truce?'

'I don't see how,' he replied, leading the last horse out of the water. 'I'm not going to give up until I find Tom Hollick. If he was part of the gang that killed my sister then he's a dead man.' He looked at her bleakly. 'Guess I'm sorry, seeing what that's going to mean to you and your brother, but nothing you say is going to change my mind.'

'I've been thinking about that,' she replied, handing him his coffee. 'If you hadn't stopped them, maybe Towse and Whip would've killed me, the way somebody killed your sister. I'll never believe Uncle Tom would do a thing like that.' She swiped the back of her hand across her eyes as her voice faltered. 'He must be dead. So you go ahead and look for him, and we'll help you, because then me and Johnny can give him a proper funeral, just like we did for Pa.'

*

The rodeo had moved on, and Dobie's Bluff had shrunk back to the hick town it had always been, dozing through the afternoon, its streets almost empty. Garvin hesitated for only a moment before he rode across to the sheriff's office. What old Marriday had said about a lawman was itching at the back of his mind. If only Simons had given him a name. As he pushed the door open he read the sign that hung upon it. Sheriff Louis Bourdell.

'Didn't expect to see you again,' the sheriff said, leaning back in his chair and looking up at Garvin, a half-smile on his face. 'Did you find old Maddy?'

'Matter of fact I did,' Garvin replied.

'So, did he tell you anything useful?' The sheriff waved a hand towards the visitor's chair, and Garvin sank into it.

'Not much. But at least we know that he wasn't involved with the gang. It seems the rancher, Simons, guessed that the stage was going to be held up, and Marriday jumped out and ran before the outlaws appeared. From what he said, it looks as if Simons recognized the man who was riding shotgun. He said something to Marriday about having been a fool, and trusting somebody he shouldn't.'

'I don't get it.' Bourdell frowned. 'Are you saying Will Simons was the reason the stage got held up?'

'Yes. Sheriff Tate told me Simons was carrying a lot of money. And it seems the rancher let that information get to the wrong person. That's what he meant by talking to Marriday about trust.'

'Unless we know who he meant, that doesn't get you any closer to finding out who was behind the robbery.'

'Maybe not,' Garvin said. 'But there was one small detail that Simons mentioned to Marriday that I haven't told you yet. He said the man who betrayed him wore a badge.'

CHAPTER EIGHT

'You better not be sayin' what I think you're sayin',' Sheriff Bourdell said, his eyes narrowing as he hunched forward in his chair.

'Just telling you what Simons told the old man,' Garvin replied calmly. 'You're not the only lawman in these parts. Matter of fact, when I mentioned it to Marshal Tate back in Sykes' Pass he was real upset. I had to leave town in a hurry.'

'Is that so?' Bourdell looked thoughtful. 'Tate's been marshal a long time. Him and Simons must go back quite a ways.'

'He wasn't inclined to talk to me about that,' Garvin said. 'But I reckon it's a waste of time pushing it; could be old Marriday got it wrong.'

'Then what are you plannin' to do now?'

'Find Tom Hollick. If anyone's got the answers it's him. His brother's kids reckon he must've been killed by the gang, but if that's so I don't know how come me and Tate and the rest of the posse didn't find the body.'

'If Tate was behind the hold-up maybe he didn't want it found.' Bourdell offered him a graveyard smile. 'It might suit him to keep you busy, looking for a dead man, and all the while the trail's growing colder.'

'Maybe, but I still figure I'll take another shot at finding Hollick. I'll track down King Mo's outfit, see if anyone knows where he's likely to be. If that don't work then I'll pay a visit to the Circle S,' Garvin replied.

'Simons's place?' The sheriff shifted in his seat, frowning a little. 'Why? You ain't likely to find Hollick there.'

'No, but if I can't track him down then all I've got left is what Simons said about a lawman. Maybe his wife or his foreman might know who it is. Won't do any harm to offer the widow my condolences anyway, that's just plain good manners. I was the one found Simons's body.'

'Well, I guess that won't hurt. If you're going after King Mo there's no point leaving now, the light's almost gone. You might as well stay in town tonight.' The sheriff pushed back his chair and stood up. 'Unless you've got other plans why don't I buy you a drink? I was plannin' to take a walk down to the Silver Spur.'

Garvin nodded, getting to his feet. 'That's real civil of you, Sheriff. Just need to see to my horse, then I wouldn't mind a beer to wash the dust out of my throat.'.

An hour later darkness was settling over Dobie's Bluff. The town was quiet, with only a few dim lights showing. The lanterns hanging outside the Silver Spur made a welcoming pool of brightness in the gloom.

Two drunks spilled out of the saloon, careening off the hitching rail and clutching at each other for support as they wove their way unsteadily along the sidewalk. Following them out through the swing doors, Cole Garvin paused to draw in a long breath of fresh air; his head was full of smoke.

The sheriff had left a few minutes earlier, claiming he

had to make his round of the streets. Not sorry to be rid of Bourdell's company, Garvin had taken his time finishing his second beer, staring moodily into his glass. The sheriff had told him King Mo's outfit had left only the day before, and he was trying to convince himself the Hollick kids would be just fine if he rode on, leaving them camped a couple of miles out of town. He'd prefer to escape from their company while he tracked down their uncle. There was no reason why the rodeo boss's trail should cross theirs, and Whip was surely going to be out of action for quite a while, yet Garvin found himself wondering if maybe he should check up on them before he went looking for the rodeo.

He turned the same way as the drunks, skirting around them to enter a dark side street, where the sheriff had assured him he would find a cheap boarding house. It was pitch-black in the narrow space between unbroken wooden walls, and Garvin slowed, waiting for his eyes to get used to the darkness.

Feeling the movement of the air rather than seeing its cause, Garvin was turning, ducking, when the object that was supposed to dash his brains out swept towards his head. His quick reaction saved his life, but the power of the stroke, dealing a glancing blow to the side of his skull before crashing into his right shoulder, was enough to knock him down. Half his body numb and his mind reeling, Garvin was on his knees. There was no feeling in his hand: he couldn't get his fingers to the butt of his gun.

Still blind in the darkness of the alleyway, Garvin sensed that his attacker was about to finish what he'd started, and he flung himself haphazardly sideways. As he rolled on the ground he knew he was only delaying the inevitable, and inwardly cursed his stupidity; coming to Dobie's Bluff to offer himself up as bait, he had failed to take even the most basic precautions. A second blow made contact, missing his head but thudding painfully across his back. Flipping over again, he found he could see his assailant, a darker shadow against the starlit sky. Struggling to force his addled brain to function, Garvin tried to locate his gun left-handed, aware that the man was moving in for the kill.

A shout echoed down the narrow alley. 'This way! Come on!'

Garvin thought he recognized the voice, though his befuddled head couldn't be sure. The figure poised above him froze, the cudgel in his hand suspended in mid-air.

'Bet you'd like another drink, there's plenty. I got a whole bottle.' It sounded like a boy. A name came to Garvin, along with the memory of a freckled face. Johnny. The kid was called Johnny. But that didn't make sense, because he wasn't supposed to be here.

There was a high-pitched laugh then, harsh and strained. A woman? Garvin screwed his eyes shut briefly, wishing he could clear his head. His questing fingers had located the butt of his six-gun. Awkward with his left hand, he struggled to pull it from the holster; another few seconds, and he might have a chance of survival.

A rush of footsteps thudded towards him, loud between the high walls, along with a drunken peel of laughter. Muttering a muffled curse the shape looming over Garvin withdrew hazily from his sight, its place taken by others that reeled disturbingly against the stars.

Somebody let out a shout of protest, sharply bitten off, then he heard the sound of flesh striking hard against flesh and a yelp, followed by a boy's voice, taut but triumphant. 'You should've kept your dirty paws off her, mister.'

Hands grabbed Garvin's arm and pulled. 'Come on, we have to get you out of here.' He tried to help but he was dizzy, not too sure which way was upright. From somewhere close by came an oath and the scuffle of feet. A loud thud was followed by the unmistakable sound of somebody spewing wetly into the dirt, and Garvin felt nausea sweeping through his own guts as the smell of stale whiskey and vomit hit him.

'Come on!' Now there were two pairs of hands hauling at him. He was dragged to his feet, staggering as if he was the one who'd drunk too much. They got him out of the dark alleyway and into the street, where the pool of light in front of the Silver Spur offered a welcome release from the darkness.

Garvin sank to his knees.

'No, you can't stop here! Johnny, you'll have to fetch the wagon. Go on, and be quick, in case he comes back.'

With a disproportionate amount of pleasure Garvin realized he could put a name to this voice too. Johnny had a brother by the name of Al. No, not a brother. Not Al, but Alicia. A feeling akin to panic rose in him. A girl. In his mind's eye he saw her, half-naked as Towse and Whip tore the clothes from her body. Was it Towse who'd hit him? She shouldn't be here, he had to get her someplace safe.

Light feet ran away from them. Garvin lifted one foot and put it to the ground, forcing himself upright, gradually aware that his arm was draped over the girl's slender shoulders. The motion set up a thudding pain, but he didn't fall; his balance was slowly returning, along with his senses.

'I can walk,' he managed huskily, easing a little more of his weight on to his own feet. 'Which way?'

'There,' she said, pointing to the edge of town.

'Johnny's gone to fetch the wagon. Do you think that man will be back?'

Garvin didn't answer: the fog in his head was only just beginning to clear. He had an idea that Towse was dead, but maybe he'd got it wrong. Reaching down to his hip, he fastened his right hand experimentally over the butt of the .45. The numbness was replaced by a fiery pain that shot all the way to his shoulder, but he refused to acknowledge it, gritting his teeth as he drew the weapon from its holster. 'Let him come,' he said.

'Maybe we should go to the sheriff,' Alicia said, breathing hard under his weight.

Garvin came to a halt and began to shake his head, stopping as the hammer blows inside his skull grew louder. Things were coming back to him. He forced himself to think, and knew for sure that it wasn't Towse who'd attacked him. He'd been laying a trap for Sheriff Bourdell. He wasn't sure, but it looked as if the lawman had damn nearly killed the bait.

'No,' he said forcefully.

'But . . .' she began.

'I said no,' he repeated, trying to pull away from her. 'Whatever you do stay away from Bourdell. We have to get out of here.'

'All right.' She got her shoulder under his arm again, just in time to stop him falling. 'I'll do whatever you want, just take it easy. Johnny will be here soon.'

They resumed their slow progress crabwise down the street, the girl looking anxiously over her shoulder.

Garvin recalled hoisting himself into the back of the wagon, but then everything slipped away from him for a while, the world reeling around to vanish down a deep dark well. He came back to his senses with warm water trickling down the side of his head. He tried to push away the hand wielding the wet rag, but his fingers were grabbed and held.

'Let me wash it,' Alicia said, her voice soft. 'I don't know what hit you but it's left a lot of dirt behind, you don't want this going bad on you.'

Opening his eyes, Garvin made out her face by the faint flicker of firelight. The events in the alleyway came back to him in a rush. The sheriff would be looking for him, and if he found the kids at the same time he would probably deal with all three of them the same way.

'Where are we?' he demanded, trying to sit up.

'Don't worry, you're safe,' she soothed.

'The fire. He'll see it . . .'

Johnny's face come into view. 'It's all right, we're in the old barn, the one next to the corral. I just checked, the light don't show outside. Don't reckon anybody's been here since the roof fell in, we had to clear away the broken shingles so we could drive the wagon in. They make a real good fire.'

Garvin subsided, allowing himself to enjoy the sensation of small warm fingers easing his shirt away from his bruised shoulder. 'I've got some liniment here,' the girl said, 'Pa used to swear by it when he had a fall. Hold still.'

He drew in an involuntary breath; the pain was bad. Alicia snatched her hand away. 'It's very swollen. Do you think the bone's broken?'

'One way to find out,' Garvin said. Gritting his teeth, he explored the bruised flesh with his left hand, the walls of the barn shimmering as his head spun again. 'Think I got lucky,' he said at last, closing his eyes to let the world straighten itself up.

'Why wouldn't you let me tell the sheriff?' Alicia asked, gently applying the liniment. 'He ought to know somebody tried to rob you.'

'That man wasn't interesting in robbing me, he wanted me dead,' Garvin said. 'And I've got a suspicion the sheriff already knows.'

'How can he?' she asked, a little frown appearing between her brows. She felt his forehead with cool fingers, as if she feared he was feverish.

'Because I think he was the man who hit me.'

'What?' Johnny exchanged worried looks with his sister. 'But it was dark, you can't have seen him.'

'Didn't need to. He wears some kind of hair-oil, it doesn't smell much better than what that drunk spewed up. Besides, I heard him swear when you two came along. It sounded a lot like Bourdell.'

'But that's crazy. Why would the sheriff bushwhack you?'

Garvin was silent for a moment, then he sighed. 'I guess because I pretty much invited him to. Marriday told me something that made me think the sheriff might be crooked, so I was giving him a chance to prove the old man had got it wrong.'

CHAPTER NINE

Garvin and the girl faced each other over the fire's ashes. It was still dark in the barn, but outside the sky was brightening.

'Do we still have our truce?' Alicia's eyes looked huge in the half-light, her thoughts impossible to guess.

'Reckon I owe you that, and more,' Garvin replied. 'I've got a feeling the two of you just saved my life.'

'There's an easy way for you to pay us back,' Alicia said quickly.

Garvin scowled. 'I won't stop looking for Tom Hollick,' he said harshly. He rubbed a hand across his aching eyes. 'I'm sorry.' His tone softened. 'I'll give him all the time it takes to tell me his story. Maybe he wasn't part of what happened to Julie, but before I let go of this thing I have to know the truth.'

'Suppose,' the girl said hesitantly, 'the outlaws didn't kill him, but he wasn't part of the hold-up?'

There was something in her tone that made him look up. 'What haven't you told me? You've been making out he's some kind of saint.'

'He broke the law once, but it was a long time ago. He's changed,' Alicia insisted. 'I heard him swear to Pa he'd never do it again.'

'Reckon I'd better hear the whole of it.'

The girl gave a brief nod. 'All right, I'll tell you. Like I said, it was a long time ago. He started mixing with the wrong company.'

'What sort of wrong company?'

'He helped some men to rob a bank. It's not as bad as it sounds,' she added hastily. 'He was training to be a lock-smith before Pa left home. Pa used to say it was his fault that Uncle Tom got into trouble, because he was the only one who could keep the peace between his brother and his father. But Pa had won a lot of money when the rodeo came to town. It was all he wanted to do. If you'd ever seen him ride, you'd understand. It was like he came to life. He . . .' she broke off to brush tears from her face.

'I saw him,' Garvin told her. 'Beat anything I ever saw.'

'Uncle Tom wanted to go along when Pa left, but Pa said he should stay and finish learning his trade.'

'But instead he argued with his father and ran off,' Garvin hazarded.

'Yes. Pa didn't hear from him after that, not for nearly three years. Then he got a message saying his brother was in jail. He'd been charged with taking part in a bank robbery. But all he did was open the safe. He had to, because he owed the man who planned the robbery a lot of money.'

'How come?'

She stared into the fire. 'He'd got too deep in a poker game. He's always been a gambler. Once he was caught he told the truth, but he still got sent to prison for five years. By the time he was freed Pa was married and settled down, breeding horses instead of riding them. Uncle Tom's pretty good with horses too, so he came and lived with us.

The trouble was, he could never make enough money to pay for his gambling debts. When Ma died and Pa took to the rodeo circuit again, Uncle Tom took off.' Alicia leant forward, lowering her voice to plead with him. 'He's not a bad man. All he ever did was open a safe. I'm sure he didn't help the men who robbed the stage.'

'It's easy for a man to turn bad,' Garvin said bleakly, ' 'specially if he needs something, the way a gambler needs money.'

'He'd never kill anybody,' Alicia insisted. 'I was thinking, about when . . .' she faltered then went on '. . . when you saved me from those men. The one called Dan didn't want me to get hurt, but he couldn't stop the others. Suppose it was the same with Uncle Tom? It wouldn't be his fault if he wasn't brave enough to help your sister.'

Garvin was silent for a while. 'I have to find him,' he said at last. 'Maybe if that's the way it was – I don't know. A man who'd stand by and watch while an innocent girl was being abused that way – he wouldn't be much of a man.'

'You told me at least three men held up the stage,' the girl replied quietly, 'if they were like Towse . . .'

Daylight was spilling through the hole in the roof, and Garvin looked at Alicia, seeing her clearly for the first time. 'He can't hurt you now,' he said. 'And I don't reckon Whip will be causing trouble for a week or two. Look, I reckon you're safest where there's plenty of people. Stay around Dobie's Bluff for a few days. I've got a couple of things to do, and I can't risk you travelling with me, if I'm right about Bourdell then he'll want to stick to me like a burr in a mustang's tail.'

'And if he does then you'll end up dead,' Alicia retorted. 'That shoulder's going to slow you down, I can see it's stiffened up this morning. Unless you can shoot left-handed we need to keep the sheriff from following you, so he can't finish what he started.'

'That's for me to worry about,' Garvin said.

'So saving your life last night was just a waste of time.' Alicia sighed. 'I suppose I shouldn't care, because if he kills you next time at least Uncle Tom will be safe.'

Garvin glowered at her. 'Bourdell's after me, and he won't have far to look. There's not much we can do that'll change that.'

'Yes there is,' she said, her cheeks dimpling. 'I've got an idea.'

'Why am I sure I'm not going to like this?' Garvin said.

It was close to midday. The wagon stood a little way out of town, pulled to the side of the trail a half-mile or so beyond the ruined barn, where a group of trees offered shade. A coffee pot hung over the meagre fire, and Alicia Hollick sat on a charred wooden box, busy with a needle and thread, face hidden by a large floppy-brimmed hat. She didn't look up as a horseman rode along the dusty trail, not even raising her eyes when he stopped a couple of yards away.

'Hello, missy. I figured that must be you. Though I didn't reckon you'd be crazy enough to come back here.'

She looked up to see Dan's round face frowning down at her.

'You know Whip's back in town?' he said. 'Dobie's Bluff ain't a good place for you an' the kid right now.'

'I thought Whip had gone with the rodeo,' the girl replied, her own brows furrowing. 'But surely we're safe enough? He was shot. He can't be fit to come looking for us yet.'

'He's healin' fast. An' he's real mad to get his own back.

I hope Garvin's got the sense to keep out of his way. An' I sure wouldn't like Whip to find you all on your lonesome neither. Ain't Garvin here? They told me at the livery that a kid fetched his horse. I reckoned I'd find the whole boilin' of you together.'

'He's not far away,' the girl replied. 'You'd better go before he gets back.'

The wrangler looked around, obviously uneasy. He narrowed his eyes when he saw the three horses that stood tethered nearby. 'Well, guess maybe I'm wastin' my time, but I'll say what I come to say.' Dan lifted down from the saddle, though he kept his distance. 'Look, I'm sorry for what happened the other day,' he said, his face pink. 'I ain't a bad man, missy, an' I don't want you gettin' hurt. That's why I figured to come here on my way out of town. If Garvin's keepin' an eye on you then I guess you'll be OK, but I heard he took a beatin', an' it ain't wise him figurin' to face Whip if he ain't at his best.'

'I didn't know about Whip,' the girl said uncertainly. 'Are you leaving for good?'

'Sure am. I worked two years for King Mo.' He grimaced. 'Liked it fine until them two turned up. Ain't much better now Towse is gone, Whip's just as bad, an' he's persuaded King Mo he needs gunslingers more'n he needs wranglers. There's a cattle drive leavin' from the other side of the river in a few days, an' I plan to be with it.'

The faint jingle of spurs announced that somebody else was approaching, coming through the narrow belt of trees to the south. Dan stood tense and watchful, his right hand gathering his reins at the saddle bow as if he was ready to mount and ride away.

Slowly Alicia rose to her feet, clutching tight at the shirt she'd been mending. She let out an involuntary gasp of pain as the needle drove into the flesh of her palm. As she stared at the growing bead of blood the rider emerged from cover. Looking up, she found herself facing the man she knew as Whip, his left arm held awkwardly across his chest, and his features twisted into an ugly grimace.

'Well, this is real cosy.' Whip eased from his saddle, his eyes flicking between the wrangler and the girl. 'You ain't the one I expected to find out here, an' that's a fact. You got yourself a little lady friend, Dan? Don't she object to that fat face o' yours, or the yellow streak you wear down your back? But then, maybe she ain't no lady. More like a cheap whore, gettin' her kicks by runnin' around dressed like a boy.'

'Leave her be, Whip,' Dan said.

'Or what?' The other man laughed. 'You plannin' to fight me, cowboy? You ain't got the guts, even though I ain't finished healin'. Tell you what, Dan, you ride on out of here, an' I'll try real hard to resist puttin' a bullet in that spineless back o' yours.'

'She's just a kid,' Dan said, standing his ground, though his voice was none too steady.

'Mount up an' ride away, yellow-belly,' Whip said, the smile wiped from his face, a raw savagery in his words. 'Go back to punchin' cows, it's the only thing you're fit for.'

With a despairing look at the girl Dan put his foot in the stirrup and lifted into the saddle. 'You're only a mile from town. There's law here, Whip, not like last time.'

'The law? You kiddin' me? You want to fetch Louis Bourdel, then go ahead, could be he'll want a piece of her too,' Whip said, glancing around the campsite. He noticed the three hoses and dropped his right hand to the butt of his six-gun. 'Where's Garvin? Him and me's got some unfinished business. Don't figure you'd be sweet-talkin' his girl if he was around, but I was told he'd be hidin' out along with Hollick's brats.'

'That's his horse right over there,' Dan replied. 'You sure you wanna meet him, Whip? Seem to recall he was the one put that slug in you.'

'Keep your mouth shut or get out of here,' Whip snarled, turning to face Alicia. 'Where is he?'

'Around,' she said. 'He's with my brother. They'll be back in a minute.'

Whip drew his gun and stepped across to the wagon, head swivelling warily. Having assured himself that there was nobody hiding there he circled the trees, then came back to prowl around the campsite. He stopped to stare at the saddle and bedroll lying close to the fire, kicking aside the blanket. A pair of boots lay hidden underneath.

'Kinda big for your brother, ain't they?' he said. The man moved back to the wagon and climbed inside. He came out a moment later with a holstered gun slung over his shoulder.

'I asked you once, an' I ain't askin' again,' Whip said. He strode across to the three tethered horses and stared at the ground as if he was looking for tracks. Then he struck the nearest animal with the hand that held his six-gun, making it squeal and shy away from him. 'Where's Garvin?'

'Not far away.' Alicia was backing nervously towards the wagon.

Whip turned to her, an ugly look on his face. 'Where is he? A man ain't travellin' far without his horse, an' he don't go leavin' his boots an' his gun behind.'

Nearly at the wagon now, Alicia glanced across at Dan, who nudged his horse towards her. 'Best tell him, missy.

Whip, you leave her be, or so help me I'll go an' shoot up the street an' fetch the whole damn town out here after me.'

'You shut up, or you'll get what's comin' to Garvin,' Whip snarled, before he turned back to the girl. 'Where'd he go?'

Alicia was pressed up against the back of the wagon. She looked from one man to the other, wringing her hands together. She swallowed hard. 'He's dead.'

CHAPTER TEN

'What did you say?' Whip advanced on the girl, and she flushed as his gaze travelled greedily over her body.

'Garvin died last night.'

Whip scowled. 'That can't be. Bourdell told me . . .' He broke off. 'What happened?'

'When he came back from town he said somebody hit him on the head. The wound was bleeding quite a bit but it didn't look like much, he wouldn't let me bandage it. He had a cup of coffee and settled down to sleep, right there by the fire. I didn't think he was badly hurt.' The girl shivered. 'When I woke up this morning he was dead. He was stone cold.'

'That's crazy,' Whip scoffed, 'a man don't just die.'

'He can so,' Dan said. 'It happened at the rodeo one time, reckon you was there too, missy. There was a fella got kicked in the head by a mustang, but he got up an' finished his ride. After that he won the ropin' competition, neat as you please. Then he dropped down dead.'

Alicia nodded. 'I remember,' she said, not taking her eyes off Whip, who was still watching her distrustfully.

'If Garvin's dead, where's the body?'

The girl pointed to a heap of stones. 'There. We buried

him, me and Johnny.'

'Without his boots?'

She flushed. 'They're good boots. They'll do for Johnny one day.'

'And what about his rifle?' Whip demanded. 'it's not in the wagon.'

'It's there.' Alicia nodded towards the fire. 'Under the wood.'

'You'd better not be lyin' to me,' Whip said, glaring at her then making for the pile of brushwood. As soon as his back was turned the girl whirled around, bending to pull Garvin's rifle from its hiding place above the axle. She put the gun to her shoulder, cocked it and took aim. 'Drop the guns,' she ordered. 'Both of them.'

'You ain't gonna shoot me,' Whip said, twisting slowly towards her, the hand that held his six-gun beginning to lift, his finger closing on the trigger. 'That thing's got a kick like a mule, it'll put you flat on your back.'

'If it does you'll never see it,' Alicia replied, 'because you'll be dead. Move your hand another inch and I'll fire.'

Whip hesitated. 'Be a shame to shoot you,' he said, his tongue flicking across his top lip. 'A real waste. I had somethin' else in mind. Reckon you don't wanna die. What d'you say?'

'She said drop the guns.' Dan's voice cut across the girl's response, and suddenly the wrangler was there, only a couple of yards away, his six-gun cocked and aimed at Whip's head. 'Gun play ain't my trade, but at this range I ain't gonna miss. Lose those irons, Whip.'

Fury etched on his features, Whip obeyed.

'Ride out, an' don't come back,' Dan said. 'An hour from now we'll be long gone, an' if you've got any sense you won't come after us.'

'Wait,' Alicia said, keeping Whip in her sights. 'Move over there,' she ordered, gesturing at the heap of stones where she'd claimed Garvin was buried. Reluctantly Whip did as he was told.

'Put your right hand down there,' the girl said. 'On the top. Dan, stay far enough away so that he can't try anything, but keep him covered.' Her face was white but there was a steely look in her eyes.

'Now hold on,' Whip protested, fear twisting his features as he looked from the girl to the wrangler.

'You sure about this, missy?' Dan asked.

'I'm sure,' she said implacably, picking up a large rock from the edge of the heap and advancing on Whip. 'Your hand.'

'That's about the worst thing I ever did in my whole life!' Cole Garvin came at a run, leaving Johnny Hollick a hundred yards behind. Away down the trail, a plume of dust rose from the hoofs of Whip's speeding horse.

Garvin strode towards Alicia, who still stood by the heap of stones she'd named as his grave. 'It was like I was stark naked, stuck out there in that arroyo without so much as a knife in my hand,' he went on furiously. 'Don't you ever do that to me again, girl.'

She dropped the rock from nerveless fingers and turned to him, her face a frozen mask. The next second she was in his arms, her head buried against his vest as her whole body shook with violent sobs.

'Hey.' He lifted a tentative hand and stroked her hair, a baffled look on his face. 'It's OK. I didn't mean it. You did real well, I swear.'

Dan stood with his mouth gaping, staring at the two of them. 'Jumpin' Judas! Mister, you sure are lively for a man who's dead an' buried. You gave me one helluva fright.'

'Wasn't you we were trying to convince, but thanks for helping out. If I'd known it was Whip she'd be dealing with I'd never have let her do it.' Garvin looked appraisingly at the wrangler over Alicia's head. 'You mean what you said about leaving?'

'Sure do. Even more reason to put some distance between me an' Dobie's Bluff now.' He lifted into the saddle. 'I'm out of here, Garvin. Hell, I thought I'd just pay a visit, make sure these kids were all right, I didn't expect to go tangling with Whip. A couple of broken fingers might put him out of action for a while, but he ain't a man to forget what he's owed.'

'I'm sorry if we lost you your job,' Garvin said, becoming uncomfortably aware of the girl, the softness of her body pressed against his, the scent of her making it hard to think straight. Gently he disentangled himself from her arms.

Dan shook his head. 'Not your fault. Never was the same workin' for King Mo once Towse an' Whip turned up, last few weeks wasn't my idea of fun.'

'Weeks? Are you saying they hadn't been with him long?' Garvin asked.

'Joined us right here in town. Seem to recall the King said it was the sheriff's idea, reckoned we might need some extra hands, with so many folks comin' in for the rodeo.'

'Keeps coming up,' Garvin murmured, 'Towse and Whip and Bourdell. I don't think much of the sheriff's choice of friends. Alicia, Johnny, start breaking camp. Reckon it's time we were leaving.'

A slight smile lifted Alicia's lips as she stared at her

brother, riding Garvin's horse up ahead of the wagon.

'Sure is nice to see the kid enjoying himself,' Dan said, reining his horse in to ride alongside.

'Reckon he'll be as good as his father one day,' Garvin said, leaning forward so he could see over the girl's shoulder.

'I just hope he doesn't end up the same way,' the girl replied, her smile fading. 'Do you really think it was the sheriff who sent Whip to look for you?'

'Looks like it,' Garvin said. He hesitated, not sure whether to voice his thought. 'I got this feeling in my gut, tells me Bourdell's tied in with the stage robbery.'

'But he's a lawman,' Alicia objected.

'Wouldn't be the first to go bad, missy,' Dan said.

'Could be he's the one who told the gang when Mr Simons was carrying a lot of money,' Garvin agreed. 'Old Marriday said Simons thought a lawman had sold him out. The sheriff could have been one of the two men who held up the stage. Maybe that's why they were so careful to leave nobody alive.'

'But you said you chased that gang for weeks,' Alicia objected. 'People would notice if the sheriff went missing that long.'

'He *had* been out of town,' Dan put in suddenly. 'Me an' one of the other boys rode to Dobie's Bluff ahead of the rest, to set up for the rodeo. When we got to town there was just a deputy in charge, real bad tempered 'cos he hadn't seen his boss in weeks. Only thing cheered him up, he reckoned the townsfolk would vote Bourdell out just as soon as they got the chance. Didn't seem to think he was doin' his job right.'

'You never heard him give any reason about why he'd been away so long?'

'Sure, whole town was talkin' about it,' Dan said. 'He claimed he'd been asked to look for three men who robbed the stage between Indian Flats an' Sykes' Pass.'

'He what?' Garvin shook his head in disbelief. 'That's a downright lie. I was riding with Marshal Tate's posse, and we never saw Bourdell, not once.' He let his gaze travel back along the dusty trail, where the wheel ruts unrolled behind the wagon. His face was bleak. The crazy idea kept returning to him. He turned to Dan again. 'So, the sheriff and Towse and Whip, they all turned up together, after you got into town?'

'Yeah, I reckon they did.'

'You happen to know if Whip's got another name?' Garvin asked. There was a pulse beating hard and fast in his temple.

'Reckon he must do, but I never heard it,' Dan replied.

Garvin shook his head, trying to chase out the half-baked notion that Whip might be Zeke Dailey. The only description they had of the man who rode shotgun wasn't much use, it could have fitted Garvin himself almost as well as Whip, and with old Marriday dead nobody was likely to give them a better one. He was clutching at straws.

Garvin sighed. The sooner he caught up with the rodeo, finished his business there and got on his way to the Circle S the better; he needed to find out just how well the sheriff of Dobie's Bluff had known Willard Simons. And there was another good reason for wanting to get clear of the wagon: the kids would be safer without him, especially if the sheriff got suspicious about his sudden death and decided to dig up that grave.

They travelled on until the sun was low on the horizon, then found a place to stop for the night.

'Exactly where are you headed, Dan?' Garvin asked, as

the two men tended the horses. Alicia was lighting the fire, while close by they could hear Johnny whistling as he gathered wood.

'White Falls. Used to work there, long time back. Closest I ever had to a home I reckon, still got a few friends out that way.'

'But you're moving on?'

'Yeah, signing on for a cattle drive. Why, what's on your mind?'

'Need to be sure they'll be safe,' Garvin replied, glancing towards the youngsters, now bickering together by the fire as it began to take hold. 'I've got things to do, and I can't take them with me.'

Dan nodded thoughtfully. 'Reckon I can help you. There's a preacher an' his wife, real nice folks. Figure they'd be willin' to keep an eye on 'em. I'd say they'd be glad of the company.'

Garvin gave a wry smile. 'Let's hope Alicia sees things the same way. Did you ever meet Brad Hollick's brother?'

'Tom? Sure, I recall he hung around the rodeo once or twice. Usually when he was broke, an' he wanted Brad to help him out.'

'I don't suppose you know where I'd be likely to find him?'

'No, don't reckon I do. It's a shame you went an' upset King Mo, 'cos there's a man by the name of Rookie Saunders works for him. Turned out him an' Tom used to ride together, long time back; real pals they were. If anybody knows where to look for Tom Hollick, reckon he's the one.'

Cole Garvin reined in his mount, staring at the great dust cloud ahead. King Mo had quite a following. A long caravan of riders, wagons and horses, more like a travelling circus than a rodeo, snaked towards the horizon. He hadn't believed Dan when the man had told him how big the outfit was. It looked like a town on the move, with a gaggle of hangers-on bringing up the rear; there were gamblers, drifters, traders and women, all choking on the dust thrown up by King Mo's procession.

He'd lied to Alicia, telling her he'd come back to White Falls and fetch her before he went looking for her uncle. It was better that way; he couldn't have his hands tied. If he found the man alive he would give him the chance to talk, but if Hollick had helped the gang there was only one way the encounter could end. Garvin tried to quieten his uneasy conscience by telling himself the girl need never know the truth.

Either way it was tough on the kids; if, unlikely as it seemed, their uncle had been unconnected with the robbers, then he was almost certainly already dead at the hands of the gang. On the other hand, if he'd been part of the hold-up, then death wouldn't be long in finding him.

Waiting until the campfires were lit, with all the travellers settling down to cook their evening meal, Garvin dismounted and led his horse to a wagon close to the end of the train. Four men sat around a packing-case, intent on the fall of the cards one of them was dealing. Nearby, a woman was labouring over a fire, and the smell of beef stew rose from the pot she was tending.

'Evening,' Garvin said, stopping at the very edge of the firelight. 'Any chance you folk can spare a cup of coffee?'

He was welcomed, as he had guessed he would be, once he showed an interest in joining the card game. When he confessed to having a few dollars in his vest pocket the gamblers insisted that he join them, and willingly shared not only their coffee but a meal. Once they'd eaten, the cardsharps proceeded to fleece their new lamb, and for the first few hands the pile of money in front of Garvin increased. After that, predictably, it began to dwindle.

CHAPTER ELEVEN

'Any of you gents know a man by the name of Rookie Saunders?' Garvin asked, as he threw in his hand.

'Sure, we know Rookie,' one man answered. 'He a friend of yours?'

'Nope, but I was told to look him up.' He rose to his feet, reaching for his money; he had only lost a couple of dollars, and he didn't think they'd want him to leave just yet. 'Can you tell me where I'll find him?'

'It ain't easy to get around this camp after dark. And you haven't even had a drink yet.' The gambler next to Garvin reached up and took him by the arm, gently easing him back to his seat. 'Why don't we send a message, ask Rookie if he wants to take a hand in the game for a while?' He beckoned to the woman, who had sat down to her own meal after the men had eaten, and was now pouring herself a generous measure of moonshine from an earthenware jug. 'No point you getting yourself lost. Besides, the King's men get kinda trigger-happy at night, but they're used to seeing Martha. Come on, woman, pass that jar over here.'

With a faint smile Garvin allowed himself to be persuaded. Strangely, his luck turned a little while they waited for the woman to return.

Many hours later, when two empty jugs lay by the men's feet, Garvin tossed in his hand, and at the same time he threw his question across the makeshift table, as if it was of no consequence. 'Any of you folks seen Tom Hollick lately?'

Rookie Saunders, who was a short, red-haired cowboy with a babyish face, let out a coyote-like yelp of laughter. He had done more than his share towards emptying the jugs, and his face was flushed. 'You lookin' for Tom? Mister, don't go wastin' your time. If he owes you money he's real good at stayin' outa sight. He's got hisself a hide-out to beat the band.' He tilted a jug to his lips then flung it down to rattle against the others. 'Hey, this one's empty. You fellas got any more?'

As the first light of dawn shone mistily from the horizon the poker game at last came to an end. Garvin nodded a farewell to his new friends, assuring them that he'd return another night and give them a chance to win back the money he'd taken off them. The moonshine had done a lot to straighten the play, as they gradually became too drunk to cheat with any conviction, while Garvin had become adept at tipping the jug without drinking. He walked away, supporting Rookie Saunders, who was hiccuping drunkenly.

His horse was where he'd left it, dozing behind the wagons. Garvin's head was spinning with weariness and the after-effects of the knock it had taken the night before. He'd have felt a whole lot worse if he hadn't managed to avoid the moonshine, but he had a raging thirst, and he emptied his canteen almost at one swallow.

Rookie didn't put up a fight when Garvin levered him into his saddle, accepting the suggestion that it would be quicker to ride round the camp than attempt to find their way through it. After climbing up behind Saunders, Garvin hooked the man's gun swiftly from its holster and dug it into his ribs. 'Sit tight,' he advised. He needn't have bothered. Rookie Saunders heard and felt nothing. The cowboy slumped forward over the saddlebow, and within seconds a low rhythmic snore rasped from his gaping mouth. With a humourless grin Garvin tucked the man's gun into the back of his own belt, and nudged the horse into motion.

Stopping now and then so that the horse didn't founder under its double burden, Garvin pushed as hard as he could towards the Circle S. He didn't know the country, but he'd memorized the map from the sheriff's office, and he thought he'd recognize the double bend in the river that had given the ranch its brand, and its name. Saunders didn't wake up until the horse was sliding down the steep bank towards the water, with Garvin at its head.

'Wha-a,' the man croaked, half-lifting his head then letting it sink again with a groan.

'Moonshine,' Garvin said, by way of explanation. 'You had way too much of it.' Once they were in the shallows he turned the horse's head upstream, following the water while the banks closed in on either side until they were riding through a steep-sided ravine. Since the river was running low, even here there were shingle beaches in places, hidden from the view of anyone passing by. Garvin found a place that was to his liking and led the horse on to dry ground, where he pulled Saunders from the saddle.

'Gimme a drink,' Saunders demanded.

'Whatever you say.' Garvin rolled the cowboy over until he was more in the water than out of it. 'Take you quite a time to drink that dry.'

Saunders spluttered and rolled, moaning a little, though after a while he lowered his head back to the river and drank. Then he sat up, clutching his head with his hands. 'Where are we? Why d'you bring me here?' He looked around. 'Hey, there weren't no river last night!'

'You need time to sober up and get rid of that headache,' Garvin said. Bending swiftly, he unbuckled the man's belt. Before the cowboy had time to protest, his arms had been pulled together in front of him and the belt was fastened around his wrists.

'Hellfire, mister, what did I ever do to you?' Saunders stared blearily up at him.

'Nothing. But I want to be sure you're here when I get back.' He took the bandanna from the man's neck and used it to tie his ankles together.

'You gonna leave me here like this?'

'There's water to drink. Be dark in an hour, I reckon. You can sleep off the rest of that booze. I'll leave you the bedroll, and the bank will give you shade once the sun comes up,' Garvin replied. 'I've got things to do. Reckon you'll feel just fine by sundown tomorrow.'

'You can't leave me here a whole damn day!' Saunders struggled against his bonds, soon giving up with a groan, his face creasing in pain. 'That was some rotten liquor. Why you doin' this?' he demanded.

'I'll tell you later, once your mind's good and clear.' Garvin took the man's gun from his belt and gave him a long measuring look. 'There's nowhere to go from here, Saunders, seeing you were too drunk to know which direction we've been heading the last few hours. Reckon once you've sobered up some you'll get yourself free, but if you go wandering about you'll likely get lost. Could be I'd never find you again, a man can get himself killed that way.

Then again, if I did happen to find you, I might be real mad about you wasting my time, and put a dent in your skull with the barrel of your own gun. Figure you don't want that, seeing the way your head must be feeling.'

Garvin guessed he had been on Circle S land for quite a while. He'd ridden through the night, while there was light enough. Now the horse was flagging, and he eased it back to a steady jog. Soon the moon would set, and both he and his mount could rest until dawn.

A pale ribbon showed up ahead, crossing their tracks. Close to, it turned into a trail, rutted over the years by a great many wheels. Unless the stars had told him wrong, it had to lead to the Simons ranch house. He turned the horse to the right and didn't argue when it slowed to a walk. As the moon dipped lower and the uncertain light began to fade, he pulled up and sought the protection of a group of scrubby trees just off the trail.

Garvin was so weary the saddle felt heavy in his hands as he took it off the horse's back. He tied the beast so it could browse, and lay down, throwing his slicker over him and falling instantly asleep.

'Well, if this ain't a strange place to find a saddle tramp.' Garvin came groggily out of sleep to feel something digging hard into his ribs. With his head and his heart pounding in unison he stared up at the silhouette of a man, outlined against the sun. It was full daylight.

'Reckon Mrs Simons has got enough troubles, without no-good saddle-bums like you coming begging,' his tormentor went on, giving him another sharp poke.

This time Garvin recognized the voice. He pushed himself to a sitting position, wincing as his shoulder protested. 'Mike! Mike Tate!'

'That's me.' The marshal looked grim. 'What the hell are you doing here, Garvin?'

'Thought I might have a word with Mrs Simons.' Garvin dug his fingers into his eye sockets, trying to rub away the headache that throbbed behind them. Then he looked up and met Tate's look, quirking one eyebrow. 'Wanted to ask her about this crooked lawman her husband said he shouldn't have trusted.'

Tate scowled at him and Garvin raised a hand in appeasement. 'Since Sheriff Bourdell did his best to kill me a couple of days ago, I've got a feeling I might already know the answer.' He paused, trying to gauge if his one-time friend was looking any less sore. 'Are you planning to make use of that gun? If you've come to arrest me for murdering old Josiah Marriday, then you'd better be ready to do more than just poke me in the ribs with it.'

With a sigh Tate returned his gun to its holster and shifted over to hunker down a few feet away. 'Don't reckon that'll be necessary. Might not be so ready to forget that knock on the head you gave me.'

Garvin removed his Stetson and turned so the marshal could see the bloody scar above his ear. 'Bourdell settled the score for you,' he said, 'I hope you're willing to call it quits, Mike, because my skull's still feeling fragile.' He ran a hand over his stubbly jaw, yawning widely. 'Any chance you've got the makings of a meal with you?'

'No. But I got something better. I got an invite to call at the Circle S ranch. Food there's pretty good, and if we get a move on there might be something left over from breakfast. Come on.' He grabbed Garvin's hand and pulled him to his feet, then gave him a friendly clap on the shoulder.

Garvin grunted in pain and the sun seemed to darken.

'Thought you said he hit your head,' Tate commented,

taking a step back and studying him with mild amusement. 'You find out anything useful?'

'I learnt not to walk into a dark alleyway on the word of a man I didn't trust.'

Tate laughed. 'Surprised you've lived this long if you only just figured that out.'

'Got a point,' Garvin conceded. 'But I also learnt a thing or two you might want to hear. I'll tell you while we ride. My belly is telling me it's keen to prise itself off my backbone.'

Garvin told Tate how he'd offered himself up as bait in Dobie's Bluff, and nearly got himself killed when the marshal took a bite. He hesitated, then went on to tell the lawman how Whip had come looking for him the next morning. 'You'll say I'm crazy, but suppose Towse and Sheriff Bourdell held up the stage, with Whip ready and waiting for them sitting on the box alongside the driver. He could be Dailey, he fits what we know about him.'

'Which isn't much. Sounds like the Hollick girl is quite something. Did she really bust a couple of his fingers?'

'Seems like it.' He stared into the distance, recalling how upset Alicia had been afterwards, and how her body had felt as she trembled in his arms. 'I'd feel happier if he was six feet under, like his friend Towse.'

'Dead men can't talk,' Tate said, giving Garvin a long look. 'There's times it's best not to be too quick on the trigger.'

'When Towse got hold of the girl it was like seeing what happened to my sister all over again.' The memory drew deep lines on Garvin's face. 'Hell, if I'm right and he was one of the men holding up the stage then that's exactly what I was seeing.'

'I ain't laying no blame, Cole,' Tate said. 'Those youngsters sure seem to get around. Wherever you go they keep turnin' up.'

'That's probably not by chance,' Garvin admitted. 'They're worried about their uncle.'

'Reckon they got cause,' Tate replied quietly. 'Seein' you're so hell-bent on findin' him.'

'You saying I'm wrong?' Garvin pulled his horse to a standstill and looked at the marshal through narrowed eyes.

Tate sighed. 'No. But men you go looking for have a way of endin' up dead. If Tom Hollick was involved in the hold-up then you got the law on your side, you don't have to be judge and jury all on your own.'

Garvin didn't answer. He rode on in silence. It had all been so simple, the vow he'd made over his sister's body; he'd thought the posse would track down the gang, but they'd failed. Which meant he'd have no peace until he'd seen the thing through for himself. The men who robbed that stage had to die.

Unbidden, another woman's face came into his mind. As they parted Alicia Hollick had begged him yet again to spare her uncle's life. There had been tears on her face. Some part of him had wanted to take her in his arms, to offer her comfort. But he'd only repeated what he'd told her before: if Tom Hollick was guilty then he had to pay the price.

Suddenly angry, Garvin put spurs to his horse and drove it up a low rise. Without a word Tate followed, coming alongside as they reached the top. Spread below them a scatter of buildings and corrals surrounded a low-roofed house.

'Circle S,' Tate said. 'Sure was a shame about Will. Got three boys growing up to take over, oldest of 'em is sixteen.

He's a good kid, and he's got a good crew to help him out, but Will's gonna be missed around here.'

'That's another good reason for running down the men who hit that stage.'

'Sure. But even if we do, it won't bring Will back. A man who gets too set on revenge can turn bitter. Don't let this take over your whole life, Cole. When we were out with the posse you told me about that little spread of yours along by River Bend. Seems to me you ought to think about getting back to it.' Sheriff Tate wheeled his mount around to the hitching rail outside the large ranch house and lit down. 'That's what Mrs Simons is trying to do, carry on as normal. Makes a difference having a family, I guess.'

Garvin frowned. For some reason Tate's words made him think yet again about Alicia Hollick.

CHAPTER TWELVE

'It's very kind of you to come and see me, Mr Garvin.' Mrs Simons offered her hand, and Garvin took it, surprised at the roughness of her palm and the firmness of her grip.

'Not at all. That was quite a meal I had in the bunkhouse, it was good of you to feed a hungry saddle tramp.'

She smiled. 'Hardly that. If I'd known you and Mike were here I'd have asked you to join me, but I suspect you were better fed with the hands.' She turned to Tate. 'Mike, I know the boys are looking forward to seeing you. Bill's trying to break a new filly for me, and I think he'd appreciate some help.'

The sheriff gave a wry smile, glancing at Garvin as if he knew he was being got out of the way. 'Sure. I'll see you later.'

'He's a good man,' Mrs Simons said, once the marshal had gone. The woman smiled again, though the sadness of her loss shone clearly in her pale-blue eyes. 'Quite a few of the local menfolk call on me now I'm a wealthy widow, Mr Garvin, including Mike Tate. He at least has the excuse of knowing me a long time. I don't object to his visits, but it makes a change to meet a man who has no interest in me, or my money.'

Garvin was surprised by her frankness, but he returned her smile. 'I'm not sure there's any polite way of answering that, you being a mighty attractive woman. Guess I've got too many other things on my mind just now.'

She nodded. 'Come and sit on the veranda, we won't be disturbed there. Mike has told me a little about you, including why you joined his posse. I was so very sorry to hear about your sister. We have bereavement in common, if nothing else.'

'One reason I'm here is to offer you my sympathy, Mrs Simons.' Garvin said.

'I appreciate that.' She looked at him candidly. 'Not a day goes by I don't think about Will, Mr Garvin. Thanks to Mike, at least I have the comfort of knowing that he died quickly. Whereas you – that poor girl . . .'

He stared out at the distant prairie. Tate had lied to her. It had been a kindness, giving her the small consolation he could never have; Julie's death, like Will Simons's, had been anything but easy.

'I'm sorry, that was insensitive of me. Things get easier in time, so I'm told,' the woman went on. 'Working helps. I have this place, my sons. I keep occupied. Mike tells me you're a rancher too.'

'On a much smaller scale,' Garvin said. 'But I've put that behind me, until this is over. I keep busy too, in my own way. I reckon the marshal's told you that. I shan't rest easy until I've seen justice done.'

'If I was a man, perhaps I'd feel the same. But Mike is concerned for you. Unlike him, you don't wear a badge. You're acting outside the law.'

'I don't lose sleep over it. Mrs Simons, like you say, Mike's a good man, but there's times when that badge of his gets in the way. You arranged it so we could talk in private, and I hope that means you're willing to help me. If I'm ever going to find out who killed my sister and your husband, I need answers to a couple of questions.'

'I'll help you if I can,' she replied simply.

'Then tell me, who knew that your husband was carrying a lot of money on the day of the robbery?' Garvin asked.

'That's one of the first things Mike wanted to know, and I can only tell you the same as I told him. Nobody on the ranch knew about the deal he'd arranged, except our foreman. Jake has been with us for years, he and his wife and children are like family to me, I'm quite certain he didn't tell anyone.'

'If Mr Simons collected the money from Indian Flats, there must have been people there who knew.'

'I understand that the manager at the bank was very discreet. Like so many people around here, he'd known Will all his life. As for the clerk, he didn't know about the money until an hour before Will collected it. There's no reason to suspect him, and Mike's sure he wouldn't have had time to organize the robbery. He's a family man too. Would he risk ruining his life by getting involved with criminals?' Mrs Simons frowned. 'There *was* something Will said before he left here that last time. I'm sure he mentioned another town, somewhere that wasn't a part of his journey. I've tried to remember, but I'm afraid I wasn't listening too hard.' She drew the back of her hand across her eyes. 'We never think, do we, when we say goodbye to somebody we love, that we may never see them again.'

'I guess not.' Garvin turned away, giving the woman a moment to recover her composure. 'This place he mentioned, could it have been Dobie's Bluff?'

She shook her head. 'It might. I really don't know. He did business there sometimes, though mostly he went to Sykes' Pass or Indian Flats.'

'Was he on good terms with Sheriff Bourdell?'

'Not particularly, he didn't much like the man.'

'So you don't think your husband would have confided in Bourdell about the money?' Garvin persisted.

'No, I don't think so.'

'How about Mike? Did he know? I gather he and your husband were friends.' The unwelcome thought came to Garvin that Tate was among the men courting Simons's widow; not to mention that the Circle S was worth a lot of money.

'They were. But you're not suggesting that Mike could have had anything to do with the robbery?'

'No, nothing like that.' Garvin assured her; Tate wasn't the only one who was prepared to lie to save this woman's feelings. He was ready to bet on Bourdell as the crooked lawman, but there was still an outside chance it was Tate who had betrayed the rancher; he couldn't afford to forget that. 'I'm asking because it's possible, if your husband told him, that somebody else might have heard their conversation.'

'Of course. I see.' She looked relieved. 'Then yes, Mike probably did know, because he argued with Will about it one night when the marshal came to dinner. He told Will he shouldn't risk carrying large sums of money without any sort of guard. Perhaps they brought the subject up again, when they were in town. If they did, who knows how many people might have overheard them.'

Garvin was silent a moment, his gaze wandering again to the prairie spreading out beyond the veranda. 'Can you think of anybody your husband would describe as an enemy? Somebody who thought they owed him a bad turn?'

'A man can't build up a place like this without making enemies, Mr Garvin, no matter how honest they are. In fact, being honest can count against you at times.'

'This would probably be something fairly recent, at a guess.' Garvin prompted.

Mrs Simons considered the question, looking solemn. 'He dismissed a man about a year ago, a drifter who rode in looking for work the previous fall. It doesn't seem likely he's involved, though he was a violent man. If Towse had intended to hurt my husband I think he would have acted sooner.'

'Did you say Towse?' Garvin stared at her. 'Would he be a tall, hatchet-faced man?'

'Yes, that's right. Do you know him?'

'I did,' Garvin replied. 'He's dead.'

'I can't say I'm sorry. Cowboys come in just about every type, Mr Garvin, plenty of them are rough and some are foul-mouthed, but Towse was one of the worst. He had a black streak running through him.'

'What did he do?'

'There was a youngster here when Towse first came to work for us. The boy wasn't bright, but he was a willing worker. All the men teased him, it was only natural, but they meant no harm, and he took it well enough. Towse was different. He was truly cruel.' She sighed. 'The boy died, swept away when the river was high. Maybe he fell, but some of the hands told us he'd been really down ever since Towse arrived. They thought he might have jumped, but nobody knows for sure. Will was angry with himself, he said he should have got rid of Towse sooner.'

The woman gave Garvin a piercing look. 'Do you know how he died?'

101

'Yes. It was in a gunfight,' Garvin replied, unwilling to confess that he'd been the one to fire the fatal shot. His thoughts were running away with him again. 'This man Towse, did he come here alone?'

'We took on several new hands about that time. Jake could probably tell you, if it's important.'

'It could be.'

'Jake will be around the other side of the barn.' She rose from her chair. 'I'll show you.'

They found the foreman alongside Mike Tate, leaning companionably on the fence and watching a boy about the same age as Johnny Hollick lead a pretty chestnut mare around the corral.

'Finished your powwow?' Tate asked good-humouredly.

Garvin rode fast, hardly aware of his surroundings. *Towse and Whip, Towse and Whip*, the two names ran through his aching head like a drumbeat, played in time with the thud of hoofs.

Jake, the foreman at the Circle S, had a good memory. He confirmed that Towse had come to the ranch alone, but that a man had come seeking him soon after. They had come to Jake together, Towse swearing to the newcomer's good character when he asked for work. Knowing that his boss was regretting taking Towse on, Jake had turned the man away. But he remembered the drifter's name. It was Zeke Dooley. When Garvin pressed him, he recalled that Towse had addressed the man by a nickname. He'd called him Whip. Applying for the job of shotgun he'd muddied the water by calling himself Dailey, but it was him sure enough.

Towse and Whip, Towse and Whip. The refrain haunted him. Towse was dead, and Whip was probably out of action thanks to Alicia, yet the knowledge brought Garvin no peace. There had been at least one more man involved, maybe two. He should never have agreed to Alicia's plan to fake his own death; when Whip rode out looking for him he should have questioned the man. He should have forced him to name the rest of the gang. By now he could have known the truth.

Garvin spurred his mount through the river, the horse he was leading balking, then dashing alongside, spraying him with water. Mrs Simons had been more than generous, lending him not only two fresh horses but a saddle for the second. She'd also provided him with food. He hadn't wanted to delay while it was prepared, but a man had to eat; for the last two months he'd almost gotten out of the habit.

While he waited Garvin had confided his conclusions to Mike Tate, and the marshal had accepted that the evidence pointed towards Whip riding shotgun on the day of the hold-up, though as yet he wasn't totally convinced that Towse had been one of the men waiting to bushwhack the stage coach before it reached Sykes' Pass.

Mike had left the Circle S, saying he'd ride to Dobie's Bluff and ask Sheriff Bourdell to help him track down Whip Dooley, just to see how the lawman reacted. Tate shrugged off a warning to watch his back, though when Garvin persisted he offered to let him ride along to keep him company.

Garvin had to refuse. He hadn't told Tate about Rookie Saunders, held captive and waiting for him on the gravel beach half a day's ride away.

Following the river as before, he got back to the spot where he'd left his prisoner. It was before sundown, as he'd promised, although it would be dark within the hour.

103

The thought of food, hot coffee and an uninterrupted night's sleep made Garvin careless. When he'd left Saunders the day before, the man had been suffering a humdinger of a hangover, and it didn't occur to him that the man might be different once he was sober.

Riding on to the narrow strip of shingle, the low sun in his eyes, Garvin realized Saunders wasn't where he'd left him. At that exact second the man launched himself from the top of the steep-sided riverbank above.

Saunders's weight hit Garvin squarely, knocking him out of the saddle, and the two men landed together in shallow water, with Garvin underneath. Saunders was small but stocky, and stronger than he looked. He didn't waste the advantage of surprise; he wrapped his hands around Garvin's neck and thrust his head under the water.

There was just time for a gulp of air. The water was less than a foot deep, and Garvin could see his adversary's face, teeth bared and jaw clenched, slightly blurred through the swirl of bubbles rushing to the surface. Saunders tightened his grip and began to squeeze.

CHAPTER THIRTEEN

The world was turning dark. The agony in Garvin's chest told him he must breathe or die. It was rage that saved him, the rage he'd held within him ever since he looked down at his sister's ravaged body. It was swelling within him now, doing battle with the pain as the final moments of his life raced by, growing into a determination that he wouldn't give in, not until he'd finished the job he'd set out to do.

His hands had been dragging in futile effort at his attacker's wrists, his efforts growing weaker with every passing second. Now he flung them up at the face above him, his fingers clawing as he reached to tear at Saunders's eyes.

Saunders hurled himself back; it was that or be blinded. Garvin used the last ounce of his strength to heave the man's weight away from him, and his head came explosively from the water, mouth gaping like a stranded fish. With a roar of anger, Saunders lunged at him again, his clawed hands groping to find Garvin's arms and hold them down, doing his best to drive his head back under water.

Garvin's greater strength kept him from going under,

until the cowboy's thickset ribcage connected hard with his skull. Again water gushed into ears and eyes, but Garvin had filled his lungs with air as he went over backwards. He took Saunders with him, using the cowboy's momentum to toss him over his head.

Once rid of his burden, Garvin managed to scramble to his hands and knees, only to feel Saunders land heavily on his back, hands reaching again for his throat. Garvin grinned savagely to himself, half in triumph and half in pain. He heaved upwards, bucking like a maddened bronco, his injured shoulder shrieking a protest. Again Saunders took flight, and this time Garvin tried to keep hold of him. If he'd succeeded the fight would have been over, for he would have borne down upon the smaller man and let him take his turn at trying to breathe under water. Somehow though, his adversary slipped from his hands, to land a few feet downstream.

For the moment Garvin was beyond pressing his advantage. He knelt in the shallows, gulping in deep painful breaths. As his sight cleared he saw Saunders on his feet, not coming back at him, but wading frantically upstream.

The horses stood at the end of the shingle beach, apparently uneasy, but making no attempt to escape the man who was plunging through the water towards them. Garvin staggered to his feet and reeled on to dry land, but the cowboy had a head start; he reached the nearest horse and leaped into the saddle. Seeing Garvin almost upon him, and with the other horse shying out of reach, Saunders turned to ride further downstream, kicking frantically at his mount's ribs.

Obediently the horse splashed towards the middle of the river, but suddenly there was nothing beneath its feet. The animal floundered, its head and neck dipping out of

106

sight, and Saunders was flung bodily from the saddle. Recovering, the horse began to swim, the current taking it quite a way before it regained the far bank. In the centre of the stream Saunders's head appeared, along with an arm that thrashed wildly for a second, before both vanished again.

Garvin's head was slowly clearing as his laboured breathing eased. He stared at the swirling water. Saunders hadn't reappeared: the man couldn't swim. Cursing, flinging off his boots and unbuckling his gun belt as he went, Garvin ran along the bank.

Garvin's long legs carried him faster than the river was running. When the cowboy eventually appeared, arms flailing in a frantic but useless attempt to keep his head above water, Garvin plunged into the stream. He took two strides then dived, his long arms tugging at the water to bring him ahead of the drowning man, who had quickly vanished from sight again.

Abruptly darkness descended. The river had run into an even narrower ravine, its waters swift and noisy, the light of the setting sun cut off by the high walls of the gorge. Garvin let himself be carried by the current, listening, straining his eyes in the gloom. Something grabbed him, tugged at the back of his vest, then entangled itself with his arm, almost dragging his head beneath the water. Kicking hard, Garvin pulled free from Saunders's desperate clutches, then dived back and grabbed the man by his shock of red hair. A squeal of pain was followed by a choking gurgle, and a breathless curse.

For long minutes they were swept down river, Garvin keeping Saunders's head above water with a firm grip on the handful of hair, while staying clear of the man's attempts to grab hold of him. Now and then he tried to

107

angle towards the side, but he could see no hope of climb-ing out of the ravine, lined as it was on each side by steep cliffs of black stone. At last the pace of the water slack-ened, and they emerged from total darkness to half-light where the river broke free from the ravine and curved around in a lazy meander. Once again there were shelving beaches of shingle, with higher banks beyond that marked the river's course when it was in flood.

Wearily Garvin dragged Saunders to dry land and dropped him. The last light was fading swiftly from the sky. Garvin calculated they must have travelled at least a mile from the place where he'd seen the horse pull itself from the water.

Saunders got to his knees, then to his feet, coming upright and turning angrily to face Garvin. 'What the hell do you want?' he yelled.

'If you hadn't jumped me you'd have found out without nearly drowning the both of us,' Garvin shouted back. 'I wanted to ask you one question, that's all. If you hadn't been out of your mind on moonshine I could've asked you before.'

'What the blazes could I know that's worth all this?' Saunders flared.

Garvin grabbed the front of the other man's shirt, his face twisting with anger. 'Tell me where I can find Tom Hollick.'

'What?' Saunders flung up his arms, trying to free himself. 'Hell, no!'

Garvin hung on, shaking the cowboy so hard his teeth rattled. 'Tell me,' he bellowed furiously. He released his grip and punched Saunders in the face, feeling a savage satisfaction as something gave beneath his fist.

Saunders fell, his broken nose spraying blood. Garvin

swooped to drag him upright, hauling him close so that their eyes were only inches apart. 'Tell me,' he said again, the words grating out between gritted teeth.

'I ain't talkin'.'

It was suddenly completely dark, and Garvin couldn't see the man's expression, though he could almost smell his fear. He turned his fist so that the bandanna he had bunched in his fist was pulled tight around Saunders's throat. 'You'd better change your mind, mister, while you still got breath to do it.'

With a tiny shrug Saunders stopped struggling, going limp in Garvin's hands. 'Don't reckon I can. Tom saved my life more'n once. Hell, one time he risked his own neck to pull me clear during a stampede. You're askin' the wrong man.' His voice was becoming strained, his throat closing under the pressure from Garvin's fingers. 'Guess you should've left me to drown.'

Garvin was breathing hard, listening to the anguished sound of Saunders's struggles for air. Some part of him wanted to pummel the man to a pulp and throw him back into the river. When Julie died, he had sworn to feel no pity, to show no mercy and acknowledge no law, until the men who killed her had paid for their crime.

Little by little Garvin's hands relaxed their grip. He had failed. Deep down he was still the man he'd been some measureless time ago; Saunders hadn't been there the day the stage was held up. He couldn't kill a stubborn cowboy whose only fault was loyalty to a friend. As his shoulders sagged, Garvin's fists dropped to his sides and he turned away.

The moon was high in the sky by the time Garvin eventually limped back to the place where he'd discarded his boots and gun belt. He was cold and soaked to the skin, facing a night with no food and no bedroll. More than anything he wanted a cup of coffee, but that meant finding the horses.

Having pulled his wet boots on to his sore feet, he looked for Saunders. The man had followed him at a distance and was now watching him warily from the back of the shingle beach.

'I'll go look for the horses,' Garvin said. 'You can ride one of them back to the rodeo in the morning, long as you find some way of sending it back to the Circle S.' Even as he said it he wondered if the animals had already run all the way home. The way his luck was panning out it seemed likely.

Working his way slowly upstream, Garvin came to the place where he'd first crossed the river. On the other side, silhouetted against the moon, the two horses were grazing. Shivering, Garvin waded back into the water, talking gently to the animals as they raised their heads to look at him, the thought of food and hot coffee making him cautious as he crept closer.

When Garvin got back, riding quietly through the shallows, he was surprised to see Saunders crouching over the flickering flames of a fire.

'My pappy taught me to always keep a flint in my pocket,' Saunders said, as Garvin dismounted. 'Any chance you got coffee in them saddle-bags?'

A couple of hours later Garvin lay back against his saddle, fed and dry, his eyes half-shut as sleep beckoned.

'You must want that money awful bad,' Saunders said, tipping the last dregs of coffee from his mug.

'What money?' Garvin opened his eyes a little.

'The money Tom Hollick owes you.'

He doesn't owe me money,' Garvin said. 'I've never even met him.'

'Then what in tarnation is this all about? I never knew anybody want Tom unless it was 'cos he owed 'em a fistful of dough. Hey, you ain't the law?' Saunders sounded alarmed. 'Tom stepped over the line one time, years gone. He served time for it. Can't see him doin' anythin' that might put him back in jail.'

'I'm not the law,' Garvin replied wearily. 'Guess I owe you an explanation.' He leant forward to stir up the fire. 'Three months ago I was running a small herd of cattle on a ranch near River Bend. Then I heard my aunt had died, back in Pennsylvania, which meant my kid sister was left all alone. I was busy, I didn't want to take the time to go back East, so I sent some money and arranged for her to come out on the stage.' Garvin sighed, staring into the flames. 'I'm never going to stop regretting that for the rest of my life.' His voice sombre, he told Rookie Saunders the rest of the story.

'You certain sure Tom was on that stage?' Saunders asked, once Garvin had finished.

'Positive. Man at the way station had met him before.'

'Then I reckon he's dead, 'cos there ain't no way he'd mess with a hold-up. An' I swear he wouldn't lay a finger on a woman who wasn't willin' neither.'

'If they killed him how come we didn't find his body?' Garvin argued.

'I don't know. Unless he got away, same as that old-timer.' Saunders shrugged. 'Don't sound likely, but it sure beats the hell out of thinkin' Tom's a murderer.' He reached to pour himself more coffee, then offered the pot to Garvin. 'Tell you what I'll do,' he said. 'King Mo can do without me a few more days. If Tom's alive and hiding out then there's only one place he'd go. I'll show you the way. Don't reckon he'll be there, but no harm in takin' a look.'

'You'd do that?' Garvin stared at him. 'If you're wrong, if he was a part of that gang, I'll kill him.'

Saunders grinned. 'Mister, on my own I ain't your match, but you'll maybe think twice about takin' on the two of us. Anyways, there's another thing my pappy taught me,' he said. 'Don't go tryin' to cross your rivers till you reach 'em.'

'Might have been better if he'd taught you to swim.' Garvin replied drily.

CHAPTER FOURTEEN

The prairie had given way to a trackless land of dust and rock, where the sun beat down relentlessly on the two riders by day, while by night clear skies brought bitter cold and left them shivering in their bedrolls.

'A man's got to be desperate to live out here,' Garvin said. They had stopped to make camp, lighting a meagre fire to brew coffee; there wasn't much to burn where even cactus struggled to find a foothold.

Rookie Saunders shrugged. 'There's water where we're going, it ain't so bad.'

'Still seems a long hard ride just to get away from a gambling debt. You never figure Hollick had more than that on his mind?'

The cowboy didn't answer, and as the stars appeared, arching above their heads, cold and distant, they wrapped themselves in their blankets and did their best to sleep as the air took on its nightly chill.

Garvin woke abruptly, staring up at the moon; nearly full, it dimmed the diamond brightness of the stars. Turning his head he could see the deep shadow cast by a pile of horse droppings. He jolted upright. In the place where Saunders had lain there was nothing but a faint outline in the dust. The cowboy's saddle and bedroll had gone. And so had both horses. Cursing, Garvin threw off his blanket, his breath steaming white in the cold.

For a mile and more the tracks were easy to follow, then suddenly his boots were ringing on solid rock, and not even a scuff mark showed which direction the man had taken. Garvin swore aloud at the unyielding ground, then at himself for being stupid enough to trust Rookie Saunders. When he'd done with that he added a few choice words on the missing cowboy and his friend Tom Hollick, until at last he ran out of breath.

It could have been worse. Garvin had taken the precaution of sleeping with the saddle-bags containing all their food, along with Saunders's six-gun, all of which had been tucked against his side, along with their two canteens. It made quite a load to carry, but there was enough water to keep him going for a couple of days at least. He guessed that Saunders had waited until they weren't far from Hollick's hideout before he made his move. All he had to do was figure out where it was.

The outcrop of rock was uneven, and in places dust had settled in shallow gullies. Hoping that Saunders had gotten careless, Garvin abandoned his saddle and bedroll to walk a wide circle around the place where the tracks disappeared, hunkering down to wait out the darkness once the moon had set. The sun was well above the horizon before he found a clear hoof print. A shod horse had passed this way, heading south-east, which was pretty much the direction Saunders had been leading him for the last two days.

As the day grew hotter a heat haze obscured the desolate landscape. Garvin walked on, keeping a steady pace. A small dark something shimmered on the ground a little way ahead, and was gradually revealed to be a pile of horse dung. Only the surface had been dried out by the sun; Saunders must have waited out the darkest part of the night. It gave Garvin a little satisfaction to know the man had no water. As he straightened up to scan the horizon he saw another larger shape, an indistinct blot that had a strange reddish tinge in that landscape of black shadows and glaring white dust. Garvin frowned, squinting into the haze; whatever it was, it appeared to be moving.

Garvin shouldered the saddle-bags and rifle and set off again, half-blinded by the brightness of the sun reflecting painfully from the dust. The sun's heat felt like hammer blows to his head. Drawing nearer, he realized there were two shapes, one low to the ground, dark and immobile, while the movement of the other was no illusion. Garvin began to run.

The horse was a bright chestnut. It turned to look at him and whinnied a greeting. Then, nostrils flaring, it took a wary step towards the man lying face down a few yards further on. Murmuring words of reassurance Garvin went to catch up the animal's rein. It followed him willingly enough, though it snorted and tried to pull back as they got closer to the man who lay so still in the dust. Two paces away, Garvin's less sensitive nostrils caught the scent of blood.

There was something familiar about the brown hat and the shabby leather vest, though when he'd last seen it there had been no hole ripped through it, high on the left side. Garvin reached to turn the body over, and found himself looking into the face of Marshal Mike Tate. The bullet had come out in his armpit, and dried blood stained his shirt sleeve, spreading out to darken the leather across his chest.

Garvin stared down at the lawman, his first swift anger followed by an unexpected feeling of regret; Tate had become a friend. He pushed the thought aside; once, a lifetime ago, he had been a man who let himself be touched by emotion. Since he'd made his vow to exact vengeance for his sister's death, it was a luxury he couldn't afford.

Retreating into the hard shell he'd grown that day, Garvin forced himself to think. Why had Tate turned up here, of all places? And who had shot him? The most obvious answer would be that the marshal had encountered Saunders, but the cowboy had been unarmed and Tate's six-gun was still in the holster at his side. Reaching for the pistol, Garvin checked that it hadn't been fired.

As he returned the gun to its place his hand brushed Tate's shoulder. The blood beneath his fingers was still wet. He lowered his head to the other man's mouth. Faint, but unmistakable, a damp warmth touched his cheek. Tate was still alive.

The tethered horse provided a tiny patch of shade. Garvin trickled water into Tate's mouth and watched him swallow. A few moments later the man's eyes opened, and he stared up at Garvin, recognition slowly dawning on his face.

'Who was it, Mike?' Garvin asked urgently. 'Who shot you?'

'Must have been Bourdell.' The cracked lips attempted a smile. 'Guess he knew I was following him all the time. Didn't even see the bastard, he must've found cover around here someplace. First I knew, I was face down and eating dirt.'

116

Garvin tipped the canteen again. 'Easy, not too much. You got any idea where he was heading?'

'He was running. Reckon you'd already got him jittery. When I turned up and started asking questions he bolted, came out to this hell-hole, steering east by south, near enough in a straight line. Don't know if that helps you any.' He clutched at Garvin's sleeve with a feeble hand. 'Get him for me, Cole. Damn back-shooting coward.'

'I'll get him,' Garvin promised, as Tate's eyes drifted shut. He put his fingers to the marshal's skin and felt his pulse. It was a little fast, but strong. Garvin bit down hard on his lip; he couldn't leave Tate to die, but the man wasn't fit to ride, and every minute he stayed with him put Bourdell further ahead. And Saunders.

Before he came across Tate, Garvin had begun to suspect that he'd been hoodwinked by the red-haired cowpoke. He'd wondered if Hollick's hideout existed. Now everything was changed. It couldn't be coincidence that Bourdell had been heading the same way.

With a stash of wood that Tate had tied to the back of his saddle, and chips of dried dung, Garvin made a fire and boiled some water, pouring it over the marshal's wound while it was still hot enough to scald. He'd heard somewhere that the treatment could stop torn flesh turning bad. Tate bit down hard on his lip but made no sound as the rough remedy was administered, but as Garvin tied on a bandage made from Tate's shirttail the marshal grew restless under his hands, trying to push him away.

'Don't waste your time,' Tate whispered. 'Bourdell was one of the men who held up the stage. If you ride fast you can catch him.'

'I can't just leave you,' Garvin protested, though his gaze wandered to the horizon. 'Once it's cooled down

117

some I'll go scout around.' If he was right about Saunders, if he had taken off to warn Hollick that Garvin was looking for him, maybe the man wasn't far away. He pushed aside the thought that it might have been Bourdell's horse, or even Tate's, that he'd been following, in which case Saunders could be many miles away, even back with the rodeo by now.

Garvin found the shallow gully where Bourdell had hidden to ambush the marshal, and moved the injured man there; it would provide him with a little shelter if he had to face another day in the relentless sun. Leaving Tate all the water he had, he propped the lawman's rifle at his side, mounted the chestnut horse and headed south-east as the sun slid down towards the horizon.

Once the moon was high, Garvin lit down from the saddle, scanning the ground for tracks, seeking some sign that he was on Bourdell's trail. As he remounted, something caught the corner of his eye. He dragged the chestnut's head around and stared into the darkness to the west. There was a light there, the flickering yellow glow of a camp-fire.

Approaching slowly and on foot, Garvin circled wide and came across two horses, tethered to a wagon. He stared at them in disbelief; there were more folks out here in the desert than in some hick one-horse towns. As he crept closer he saw two figures sitting by the fire, one a lot larger than the other. The smaller one leant forward to throw more wood on the flames and the light shone clear on his face. It was Johnny Hollick.

'Why the blazes aren't you in White Falls?' Garvin yelled, storming into the camp. Taken by surprise, the man who sat at the boy's side leapt to his feet, a six-gun appearing in his fist. Garvin threw up his hands in mock surrender, impressed by the cowboy's speed. 'Hey, Dan, hold on. Guess I should've made more noise on the way in.'

'You! Hell, I thought it might be the sheriff.' Dan lowered the gun, huffing out the breath he'd been holding. 'Never thought we'd find you in these parts.' He holstered his pistol and sat down.

'Same goes for me,' Garvin said. 'Don't go getting comfortable,' he warned. 'I didn't think I'd ever be glad to see these youngsters out here, but this wagon of theirs is sure a welcome sight.'

'You might change your mind when you know why we're here,' Dan broke in. He dug around in his pockets as if he was searching for something.

'What do you mean?' Garvin asked. He looked at the wagon, surprised that their voices hadn't roused Alicia. Feeling fear tug at him, he looked at Johnny. 'Where is she?' The boy merely shrugged and went back to gazing into the fire.

Garvin turned to Dan. 'What happened?'

'Women!' Dan spat expressively. He produced a crumpled piece of paper from inside his vest. 'Damn fool girl left that for me, before we even got as far as White Falls. I couldn't make it out, but Johnny here knows his letters, an' he figured it.' He handed the note to Garvin. 'There was twenty bucks with it.'

this is fer yor horse I wul bring him bac reel soon. Al. Garvin read. He stared at the man and the boy across the fire. 'You let her go?' The words exploded from him, his fists clenching as he sought for some way to express his rage.

'What was I supposed to do?' Dan asked sullenly. 'Leave the kid in the middle of nowhere an' ride after her bare-ridged on one of them?' He tipped a thumb towards the wagon team.

'You're following her trail?'

'No need,' Johnny Hollick said. 'I know where she's going.'

'You have to tell me,' Garvin insisted. From the moment they'd finished hitching the team and set off he had ridden alongside the wagon, arguing with Johnny. The stubborn set of the boy's mouth reminded him powerfully of Alicia. For the second time that night he felt the dangerous tug of emotion, and did his best to ignore it. Like the time when he'd seen the girl at the mercy of Towse and Whip, he told himself he was only feeling that way because she was young and innocent, like his sister.

'I promised.' Johnny said.

'Kid, there's times when a promise just ain't worth nothin' no more,' Dan put in, clucking to the horses to speed them up.

Garvin looked at the round-faced cowboy in surprise; he hadn't expected Dan to be on his side. 'He's right,' he said. 'Could be Sheriff Bourdell is at Hollick's hideout right now.'

'Uncle Tom won't let nobody hurt Al,' Johnny said, though he didn't sound too sure.

'Suppose Whip turns up too,' Dan turned earnestly to the boy. 'After what your sister done, he ain't gonna be happy till he gets his own back. She'll likely get herself killed. You was ready to take me along, so why not tell Garvin where he has to go.'

'I promised,' Johnny said, anguished now. 'Al said I mustn't.'

'Listen, Johnny,' Garvin said, the words pouring from him almost against his will. 'I'll make *you* a promise. For Alicia's sake. If you tell me the way to Tom Hollick's hide-

120

out I swear I'll do my best to bring him in alive. I'll hand him over to the law. I won't kill him, not unless he gives me no choice.'

'You mean that?'

Garvin stared at the boy, all pretence forgotten. 'I mean it.' Seemingly it wasn't so easy to build a wall and stay behind it. Stone crumbled, wood rotted, and when they fell a man could still get hurt. He cared about Alicia Hollick. Julie was dead, and nothing could change that. What mattered now was keeping Alicia alive and whole.

Up ahead he could see the place where he'd left Mike Tate; if the marshal lasted through the night he'd maybe make it back to Dobie's Bluff with Dan and Johnny's help. He listened carefully to what the boy had to tell him, then wheeled Tate's horse and swept back with his heels.

'Take good care of them, Dan,' he shouted. 'I'll see you in Dobie's Bluff.'

CHAPTER FIFTEEN

Without directions Garvin doubted if he would ever have found Hollick's hideout. Thanks to Johnny he was able to follow an invisible trail across the wilderness of bare rock, where there were no tracks to follow, hardly a hint that men had ever been that way before.

When he judged he was close, and mindful of the boy's warning that it was hard to approach unseen, Garvin left the chestnut hidden among rocks and continued on foot. He removed his hat and smeared his face and hair with dust before he crept slowly up the last slope, then he slithered the final few paces on his belly, until he could see over the top. With the sun beating hot on his unprotected head he lay studying the little cluster of buildings below, trying to figure out what to do.

The water hole lay well hidden in a hollow, a shrunken pool surrounded by grass and a few scrawny trees, a haven of sun-bleached life amidst the waste of stone and wind-driven dust. There were two adobe dwellings, both so old it looked as if their walls had been sculpted from the naked rock by the wind. To one side of the larger building was a small hut made from rusty metal sheets, squat and windowless, while on the other, five horses and a mule were tethered under a thatched lean-to, dozing in the afternoon heat.

Five horses, four people, Garvin calculated. Alicia had taken Dan's horse, and he recognized the two Circle S mounts brought there by Saunders. The others must belong to Tom Hollick and Sheriff Bourdell. Garvin felt an uncomfortable itch between his shoulder blades that might not have been caused by a trickle of sweat; with all the other surviving members of the gang gathered here by the water hole it was more than likely that Whip planned to join them. He turned his head to take a quick look around, wishing Marshal Tate had been fit to bring along, or even Dan. Among so many enemies it would be hard to watch his own back.

Apart from the animals there was no sign of life, although the doors of the ancient-looking houses stood open, yawning blackly at him. He eased back down the slight slope to get off the skyline, then worked his way around the hollow; it might be possible to creep closer to the other side, though he had to be careful not to let the horses catch his scent.

The adobe houses presented a blind face to the rear, and although the slope was steep and rocky Garvin thought he could find a way down there in the darkness. He sought out a place where a small outcrop of rocks offered a little cover. There was barely time to settle himself in his lookout before two men came out of the larger cabin and busied themselves carrying water to the animals. He recognized Saunders's stocky figure. As for the other man, despite the faded hat pulled low over his eyes, he looked enough like his brother for Garvin to be sure he had at last caught up with his quarry. He had been right, Tom Hollick was very much alive.

As the men finished their chores by dipping a watercan and a coffee pot into the water, Alicia came out of the smaller adobe hut to join them. In the heat she had discarded the large man's shirt she usually wore, replacing it with something more feminine; perhaps she felt safe in the presence of her father's brother.

Although Alicia's blouse was buttoned demurely to the neck it showed off the swell of rounded breasts just ripening into womanhood. She was bareheaded, and her hair lay over her shoulders like a shawl, barely dimmed by the ever-present dust. Even seeing the girl at a distance through the heat haze, Garvin couldn't help thinking how beautiful she was; Saunders stared at her so hard he tripped over his own feet and spilled some of the water from the can.

They all went together into the main building, and as the sun reached noon, then began to slide slowly towards the west, the little settlement lay in drowsy silence, while Garvin kept watch and felt his flesh scorching through his clothes.

From a state perilously close to sleeping, Garvin suddenly jerked awake. Down below, one of the horses had been saddled. As he watched, Saunders brought out more gear. It looked as if he was planning to leave, taking both the Circle S horses with him. Tom Hollick stepped out of the adobe shack and stood leaning against its weathered wall. Garvin could hear the sound of his voice as a murmur through the thick afternoon heat, but he couldn't make out the words. With the horses ready, Saunders came to slap his friend cheerfully on the shoulder.

Garvin watched, not sorry the man was leaving; he had already bested Rookie Saunders in a fight, but he would have enough on his hands with Hollick and Bourdell.

Besides, he felt no animosity for the cowboy, who could have smashed his head in with a rock rather than simply taking his horse a couple of nights back. The wrangler had kept faith with his friend, maybe he still didn't know the truth; maybe, like Alicia, he refused to believe Hollick was involved with a gang of murdering thieves, even with the evidence right under his eyes.

As Saunders put his foot in the iron Bourdell came bursting from the old house. He grabbed the wrangler by one arm and swung him around, then planted a ferocious punch below his breast bone. Saunders doubled over, half-lifting his hands in a feeble attempt to defend himself, but he failed to block the jab that Bourdell aimed at his face. Blood spurted spectacularly from a cut above Saunders's eye, and he was falling, his knees buckling. Bourdell followed up with another vicious blow, an uppercut that snapped the wrangler's head back. It was all over for Saunders, who was crumpling to the ground, but it seemed Bourdell hadn't finished with him. He drew back his arm to deliver another blow, his murderous intention clear.

Hollick had barely moved; the attack had been so swift, so savage, he'd barely had time to react. Now at last he leapt to fasten both hands around Bourdell's taut wrist. Flinging his much slighter weight against the sheriff, Hollick managed to deflect the blow and push him off balance.

Bourdell snarled a curse. Even as he fell he battered at Hollick's head with his free hand. Pulling free as they landed sprawling in the dust, he rolled away and on to his feet with the speed of a cat, moving in to send his boot thudding into Hollick's belly.

'Stop it!' Alicia Hollick's scream reached Garvin's ears

as she came darting from the adobe shack, a rifle in her hands. 'Get away from him,' she went on desperately, as Bourdell swooped down to grip Tom Hollick by the throat. 'I mean it, I'll shoot.'

Reluctantly Bourdell straightened, eyeing the girl warily as he stepped back. There was total silence, so deep that Garvin could hear the man's next words as clearly as if he stood beside him. 'I told him nobody was to leave,' he said, thrusting an accusing finger at Saunders. One hand massaging his belly, Hollick rose to his feet, taking a few unsteady steps to reach his friend. Saunders stirred a little as Hollick hunkered down beside him.

'He asked for it.' Bourdell said, shrugging his shoulders.

'You didn't need to do this,' Hollick lifted the injured man's arm over his shoulder and heaved him upright. 'Al, put that gun down and give me a hand.'

'I don't see why we have to do what he says,' the girl replied, still keeping Bourdell covered.

'You got no choice,' Bourdell said, his lips curling in a humourless smile, 'unless you're gonna pull that trigger and finish me right here and now, but you better bear in mind I'm wearing a badge. You kill a lawman and you'll be hunted down, girl, no matter how long it takes. You'll have to run for the rest of your life, and then you'll be strung up from a tree. Being a female won't make no difference, reckon it'll just bring out the crowds. How d'you reckon you'd like that, huh? Hundreds of men comin' to watch you choke your life out, watching your legs kickin' an' that purty little face all swole up an' turnin' black.'

Hollick spoke again. Garvin couldn't hear what he said, but, her shoulders sagging, Alicia lowered the gun and turned her back on the men, to go into the smaller shack and slam the door behind her.

'That's right, girl!' Bourdell gave a harsh laugh. 'Save yourself for Whip, he's sure lookin' forward to seein' you again. Reckon he'd be here by now if that damfool doctor in Dobie's Bluff had knowed his business.'

'Bourdell,' Hollick protested, 'The girl. You swore . . .'

'Just joshin',' the sheriff replied, turning to begin unsaddling the horse. 'You gotta be able to take a joke.'

Hollick made no reply, though the look on his face told its own story. He was afraid of Bourdell. With a small shrug he helped his friend inside. Soon Bourdell followed, and silence descended again, except for a buzzing of flies around the stain where Saunders's blood was soaking into the dirt.

Garvin dared not sleep. He watched the moon climb high in the sky, casting a bright light on the tiny settlement, and waited out the long hours as it sank back towards the horizon. At last, when only the faint glow from the stars illuminated the scene, he stood up and worked some warmth back into his muscles, before slipping over the lip of the hollow and heading downhill.

He had no firm plan in his head; he knew only that Alicia was in the smaller house, and that Whip could be here any time. As for the men in the other cabin, he must hope they were sleeping soundly. Hollick must have taken part in the hold-up, but Garvin didn't think the man would try to stop him taking Alicia away. If necessary he would deal with Bourdell, though he'd prefer to get the girl to safety before he took on the renegade lawman; Alicia was far too sassy for her own good.

Treading carefully on the rough steep slope, Garvin made it to the back of the biggest building, the thick wall solid and still slightly warm as he leant against it. He held his pistol in his hand, and now, with infinite care, he pulled back the hammer. The metallic click seemed loud in the silence, but he waited through several breathless moments and no sound came to his ears.

Garvin edged his way round the house, then froze. He'd been wrong: somebody was moving. There was the slightest scrape of wood on stone. A door was opened and closed. Then came the jingle of harness, swiftly muffled, and a quick indrawn breath. Lowering himself to his knees, Garvin crawled towards the lean-to and peered round the end wall. He could see only the barest hint of a darker shadow, but the noises told him somebody was saddling a horse. The dim shape wasn't small enough to be Alicia; he couldn't be sure if it was Hollick or Saunders who worked there so swiftly and quietly.

Garvin's first thought was that Saunders wouldn't risk trying to leave again after the beating he'd taken, but then he recalled the wrangler's stubborn courage when he'd tried to make him reveal Hollick's whereabouts. With the wide spaces of the desert to lose himself in, a man wouldn't need to get far to be sure of evading Bourdell. It looked like Rookie was about to take his chances.

The horse's hoofs made little sound as it was led away up the slope. A creak of leather told him the man had mounted, and a curse muttered in a familiar voice confirmed that his guess had been right; it was Saunders. Garvin watched as the fugitive was briefly silhouetted against the sky, then he vanished down the other side of the slope. Garvin stood up. As he walked cautiously towards the smaller shack, he tried to think of a way of rousing Alicia without waking the men. He paused, his back to the rough adobe wall. The girl wasn't stupid, she would have barricaded the door in some way.

One of the horses shifted restlessly, and Garvin smiled to himself. That was it. Four horses and a mule wouldn't make much of a stampede, but the noise would surely wake Bourdell and Hollick. The men would have to go after their mounts or risk being trapped in the middle of this stony wilderness. By the time they got the animals rounded up, he'd have Alicia safely out of reach, on the horse he'd left hidden not far away.

Garvin retraced his steps. What stopped him in his tracks he hardly knew, but he froze as he reached the lean-to where the horses stood, holding his breath and feeling a cold sweat breaking out on his forehead.

The door of the larger cabin slammed open, pieces of half-rotten timber splintering, and the horses neighed their anxiety as a man plunged in among them, flinging a saddle into place. He fastened the cinches in a second and grabbed at a rein. A second, smaller figure appeared, a lighted lantern in his hand. 'Let him go, Bourdell. He won't talk, I swear it.'

The sheriff's reply rang harsh through the night as he leapt on to the animal's back and spurred away up the hill. 'Try to stop me and you're a dead man!'

CHAPTER SIXTEEN

Tom Hollick hesitated for only a second, then he hung up the lantern and ran back into the house. He came out carrying a rifle. Not bothering with a saddle, he untied his horse and threw himself on to its back, but before he could ride away a human whirlwind came flying from the smaller dwelling to grasp at his reins.

'No!' Alicia shrieked. She was dressed only in a man's nightshirt, which flapped around her legs, and she glared up at him, eyes blazing. With her teeth bared and her long hair whipping about the horse's head, she was like a figure from a nightmare, yet she had an animal beauty that made Garvin's heart race.

Scared by the sudden arrival of this apparition, Hollick's horse snorted, stepping backwards as it tried to escape. The girl clung on, although the horse's attempt to free itself swung her clear off her feet. 'You're not to go! You heard what he said!' When her uncle made no answer her tone softened, becoming a desperate plea. 'I can't bear it, not after Pa. Please.'

'Let go, Al,' Hollick replied calmly. 'You were right about Bourdell. I'm sorry, I should've listened to you yesterday. But it's not too late. I'm not playing his game any more, I ain't gonna let that bastard kill the only real friend I ever had. Rookie an' me go back a long ways. You wait right here, everything will be just fine. I'll deal with Bourdell. Hell, I'll shoot him in the back if I have to.'

Alicia shook her head. 'You won't have a chance against him, you're not a gunman,' she persisted urgently. 'Even Pa could beat you in a shooting contest, remember? It's real dark out there. Maybe Rookie already got away.'

'I don't have time to argue. Let go. I ain't gonna tell you again.'

Still she stood her ground, her lips set, her expression defiant. Suddenly Hollick kicked out with his foot, his boot heel hitting the girl hard on the arm. As her grip slackened he clapped his heels to the horse's sides and pulled its head round, tearing the rein from Alicia's hands.

The girl stamped her foot. 'No!' she screamed again, watching him ride away, tears of pain and frustration in her eyes as she rubbed at her bruised arm.

'Best thing you can do is get out of here,' Hollick called back, pushing his horse to a fast lope as he headed up the slope. 'Get as far away as you can while you got a chance. Go find your brother.'

'He's right,' Garvin said, stepping out into the lantern light. He reached to gather her to him but she backed away, her eyes sparkling dangerously.

'You! Keep away from me,' she said wildly. She glanced at the slope, seeming reassured when she realized Hollick was out of sight. 'How did you get here?'

Garvin let his hands fall to his sides, battening down on the feelings aroused by the sight of her. In her tussle with the horse, Alicia's nightshirt had fallen down to reveal an expanse of creamy white shoulder and the swell of her

131

breast. At another time, in some other place, he would have acknowledged just how much this woman meant to him.

'Your brother told me where to find you,' he said, half-turning as if he thought Hollick or Bourdell might return, finding it easier not to look at her. 'There's no time to talk; your uncle's right, you have to leave, right now. That's why I'm here.'

The crack of a shot echoed in the distance. Garvin bit back a curse. It didn't sound like a rifle, which meant Bourdell had probably caught up with Rookie Saunders. They were running out of time. He untied one of the two remaining horses and thrust the rein into Alicia's hand, then grabbed her and threw her on to the animal's back before she had time to protest. 'I'm willing to bet Brad Hollick's daughter can ride well enough without a saddle. Head south a while before you turn back towards Dobie's Bluff; it's likely Whip's coming, and you don't want to meet him. Ride fast and you'll catch up with the wagon by noon.'

'Johnny promised he wouldn't tell!' She was furiously angry, her cheeks red. 'If you think I'm leaving you here to kill Uncle Tom . . .' She tried to get off the horse, but he pushed her back.

'I won't touch him, I swear.' As he spoke Garvin dragged the horse's head around and led it up towards the lip of the hollow. 'That's why Johnny agreed to tell me the way, because I promised I'd let the law deal with your uncle. If he's innocent he's got nothing to fear from me.'

There were tears in her eyes again. 'But Bourdell said he'd kill him.'

'I heard.' Garvin increased his pace, eager to get her away. 'Get out of here, and I'll do what I can to keep him alive.'

They were at the top of the slope and still she hesitated, the horse circling restlessly. 'Why?' she demanded. 'What made you change your mind?'

'You!' Garvin slammed a fist into his palm, suddenly furious but not knowing why. 'Dammit, ever since I saw you sitting on top of that barn at the rodeo I've had no rest.' He glanced up and saw her staring at him, her face flushed, a look in her eyes he'd never seen there before. Half-turning, meaning to leave her, he swivelled back, somehow finding the words he had to say.

'I never felt this way about a woman before, Alicia. Fact is, I can't bear to let anything hurt you. I'll do what I can to save your uncle, for your sake, even if he's a killer. Move,' he ordered, slapping the horse on the rump. 'The longer you keep me here the more chance Bourdell has of putting a bullet in Hollick's hide. Now go!'

With a sound between a moan and a wail she finally obeyed him, hair flying and shirt flapping as she galloped away, sitting the speeding horse as if she was born to it.

Keeping ears and eyes open, Garvin headed for open country, trying to figure out which way the men had gone. Another shot blasted through the silence, much closer this time, and he angled towards the sound, crouching low, drawing his six-gun, his thumb on the hammer.

With nothing but the faint light of the stars to show him the ground beneath his feet, Garvin almost fell over the body that lay abandoned in the dust. Taking a quick scout around to check that he was alone, he stooped to roll the man over. Rookie Saunders stared sightlessly up at him, a great gaping hole where his nose and mouth had been; the bullet that killed him had smashed through the back of his skull and removed the lower half of his face. Once again, Bourdell had shot his victim from behind.

Garvin knelt beside the body, feeling around in the dark; the wrangler wore no gun. He swore softly; Bourdell was an unscrupulous bastard. Garvin stood up and stared into the darkness, unsure what to do. If it hadn't been for Alicia he might have gone back to his horse and ridden away, but he couldn't do that. Even if Tom Hollick had taken part in the hold-up, he'd given his word to protect him from Bourdell.

Chewing on his lip, Garvin hesitated. He still didn't know which of the gang had killed his sister. He'd vowed to bring her what peace he could, by dealing justice to her killers. Bourdell would never talk, and Garvin had a suspicion that Whip was just plain crazy; he'd trust nothing that came from that man's mouth. If he was ever to know the truth that only left Hollick. He turned and crept cautiously into the darkness. There was a small noise, a metallic click that was vaguely familiar. In the time it took for him to draw breath Garvin realized it was the sound of a rifle misfiring, and it was followed by a wild bray of laughter that echoed across the desert.

'You really think I'd risk leavin' you a loaded gun?' It was Bourdell, crowing his triumph. 'Guess it's too dark for you to see what I done.'

'Where's Rookie?' Hollick's voice came to Garvin through the night and he began to run, trying not to make any noise, guessing he was nearly out of time.

'He ain't far away,' Bourdell was saying, 'but there's no point you goin' lookin' for him. You figure there's any coyotes out here? Or vultures maybe? They're in for quite a meal.'

'You bastard!' Hollick's voice cracked. 'He wasn't any threat to you, you could've let him go.'

'That ain't my way,' Bourdell said flatly. 'I don't leave witnesses.'

'You didn't kill me,' Hollick said wildly. 'All the rest of them on that stage, but not me. That poor little kid, the driver, all the other passengers. . . . Guess you thought it was funny, dragging me along and making me watch what Whip and Towse did to that rancher.'

Bourdell laughed again. 'You shoulda seen your face when I told you it was your turn next! Your trouble is, Tom, you ain't smart, or you'd know you was safe enough. Man like you's worth too much to hand over to Whip. I just didn't want you tryin' nothin'.'

'You didn't give me much chance, keeping me hogtied—'

'Quit moanin',' Bourdell ordered, his tone suddenly changing. 'You're alive an' kickin', ain't you? Come on, we'd best get back before that girl gets ideas into her head. Don't reckon your brother kept a tight enough rein on his kids. She need breakin' in.'

Garvin's fist tightened around his .45. He had crept close enough to see the two men now, Hollick with the useless rifle in his hands, Bourdell a few paces away, sliding his pistol back into its holster.

'You hurt her and I'll never open that safe for you,' Hollick said. 'I swear it. You keep Whip away from her.'

'That ain't the way it works,' Bourdell said softly, his teeth showing as he smiled. 'I need Whip almost as much as I need you. See, I kill when I have to, but he does it because he likes it, an' that's real useful. Now, you want to keep that little girl alive, you'd better tell her to be real nice to Whip from now on. He ain't gonna be gentle, not after she went an' broke his fingers, but I reckon he'll come around, so long as she treats him right. An' when we get to the bank, you'll want to be thinkin' about that little girl, because she'll be hidden away someplace real safe. If anythin' goes wrong, if me an' Whip don't make it back, she won't never see the light of day no more.'

With an inarticulate cry Hollick launched himself at Bourdell, lifting the rifle above his head to use as a club. The sheriff brought his six-gun from its holster with lightning speed, but he didn't fire. He stepped forward to meet Hollick's attack, ducking easily under the flailing stock of the rifle and jabbing his gun hard up into his opponent's face, his other hand reaching to swipe the weapon from Hollick's slackened grasp.

As Hollick fell, Garvin took a couple of steps closer. He raised the .45 with slow deliberation, sighting it on Bourdell, keeping a tight rein on his fury. He had heard enough. This man had been responsible for Julie's death, although his tame butchers, Whip and Towse, were the killers who had made her last moments of life such a terrible ordeal.

He wrapped his finger around the trigger. Then he froze. Something cold and hard drilled into the small of his back.

'You're awful lively for a dead man,' Whip said.

CHAPTER SEVENTEEN

'You ready to die again?' Whip asked, his voice husky. 'It'll be for real this time. But if you ain't in any hurry, I'm willin' to wait awhile. You can drop the gun, and maybe we'll talk it over.'

Garvin gritted his teeth. There'd been nobody to watch his back, and yet again luck hadn't played out his way. He was left with only two options, and he didn't like either of them. He could shoot Bourdell, who stood as if frozen, knowing he was in Garvin's sights. But as he pulled the trigger, Whip would kill him.

Then there was the alternative. He could obey Whip, and put himself in the hands of a man who enjoyed inflicting pain. Garvin suppressed a shudder, recalling Willard Simons's body. A quick death would be preferable; if he gave himself up his last hours would be a living hell. But then, as long as he stayed alive there was just a chance that he might find some way to escape.

If justice was to be done, both Bourdell and Whip Dooley, alias Zeke Dailey, had to die. He spared a quick glance for Hollick. The man was kneeling on the ground, his hands held over his bloody face; he wasn't badly hurt. By now he must be wishing he'd taken a stand against Bourdell while he still stood some chance of success. While he wouldn't be much of an ally, he'd be a whole lot better than nothing.

'Well?' Whip prompted, grinding the gun barrel into Garvin's back. In reply, Garvin let his pistol drop from his hand.

Bourdell straightened, breathing hard. 'Shoot him,' he said bluntly.

'Hell no,' Whip replied easily. 'I ain't had me no fun in weeks, an' I don't figure you'll let me lay a finger on that yellow-belly you got there. Don't you worry none, I'll keep Garvin safe enough.'

'We're leaving in four days,' Bourdell said. 'That shipment will only be in the bank for a week. I've been planning this job too long to see you mess it up.'

Garvin could almost hear the smile in Whip's voice. 'I ain't messin'. Four days'll be just plenty. Start walkin', mister. An' don't try nothin', unless you want a slug in your leg. Reckon I wouldn't mind watchin' you crawl, but it sure won't make you feel no better.'

There was a growing light in the eastern sky when they got back to the hideout, where the lantern still glowed dimly by the lean-to. The solitary horse neighed a greeting and Bourdell leapt from his mount to storm through the buildings. He came back to Garvin, his face dark with rage, the six-gun in his hand pointing at Garvin's chest. 'Where did she go?'

'Guess she got tired of the company,' Garvin replied. 'Can't say I blame her.'

Whip grabbed hold of Garvin's hair and pulled, jerking his head back until he was forced to his knees. With

Bourdell now drilling the barrel of the gun into Garvin's neck, Whip put a hand either side of Garvin's head, his thumbs pressing hard at the side of his eye sockets. 'Talk,' he said. 'You ever see a man's eyes pop right out of his head?' He laughed, increasing the pressure. 'It ain't a pretty sight. You'd better squeal real quick, or you'll see it from the inside.'

Garvin hesitated, knowing Bourdell would be suspicious if he capitulated too soon. His breathing became ragged as Whip squeezed harder.

'Last chance,' Whip jeered.

'No, wait,' Garvin said hastily, trying to hide his fury with the semblance of fear. 'I told her to ride east. I guessed you'd be coming, and I figured that was the safest way to go. She'll be heading for the Circle S.'

'Why there?' Bourdell asked, leaning down to stare into Garvin's face as Whip's thumbs gouged deeper. Garvin swallowed hard. His sight was blurring. 'Because when I told Mrs Willard about the Hollick kids she said she'd take them in. She said they could stay at the Circle S until Johnny was old enough to work. I borrowed a horse so I could go fetch them, but Rookie Saunders stole it. That's the truth, I swear.' His head was a blaze of agony, and the lightening sky was growing dark.

'He's lyin',' Whip said. 'Hell, he don't need two eyes. Reckon I'll have one of 'em.'

'No. It makes sense.' Bourdell replied. 'There's no time for your games now, we have to find the girl.'

Whip gave his thumbs a vicious twist, then flung Garvin to the ground. Garvin gasped, the pain so great that he thought for a moment Whip had carried out his threat. He blinked rapidly, and almost sobbed with relief when he realized he could still see, though his vision was tinged with red.

Bourdell had gone into the cabin, now he came back and grabbed Garvin's arm. Something cold and hard was forced around his wrist, then the other arm was pulled to meet it behind his back. When Whip dragged him to his feet his hands were manacled.

'Reckon you're gonna miss bein' a lawman,' Whip sniggered. 'Them things is real handy.'

'Shut up an' get him inside. I'll deal with Hollick,' Bourdell replied.

Whip pushed Garvin towards the tiny hut made from sheets of rusty metal. Inside, he fastened a chain through the handcuffs and over the solitary wooden beam that supported the roof, pulling it tight so Garvin was held with his back bent almost double, his feet barely keeping contact with the floor and his arms dragged high above his head. 'You'd best hope we find that girl real soon,' Whip said gleefully. 'You don't look too comfortable.' He backed out, and Hollick was thrown in through the doorway, his arms and legs bound, and his wrists lashed to his ankles behind his back. Once the door was pushed shut, Garvin heard the two men hammer wedges under the door, and drag something heavy against the thick slab of wood. A few minutes later the sound of hoof beats told him the men had ridden away.

It was full daylight outside, but the only light in the hut came from a small hole in the roof. Garvin tried to move, flexing his legs a little; the pain in his arms and shoulders was bad already, and he knew it would get much worse. Even breathing was difficult. By pushing up on his toes he got a few seconds relief, but after a while he lost his balance and his full weight fell on his shoulders; it felt as if his arms were being torn from their sockets.

'Hollick,' he said, seeking for some way to distract

140

himself from the growing agony. 'Can you move?' With a flash of hope he remembered something. Whip hadn't searched him. 'Hollick, there's a knife in my boot.'

'Reckon I can get to you,' Hollick replied. There was a faint shuffling sound. 'Could take me a while. Hell, these ropes are tight, guess I'm lucky Bourdell only had one set of handcuffs. You makin' out all right?'

'I've been better,' Garvin admitted. 'How about you talk to me? Tell me what happened on the stage from Indian Falls.'

Hollick made a strange sound, half-laugh, half-sob. 'Al told me you were looking for me. Said you wanted to kill me.'

'I had it in mind,' Garvin said, 'but I guess I got you wrong. Figure maybe now's your chance to tell me your side of the story.'

'Why not.' Hollick's voice was strained, his words almost lost in the sound of his attempts to move across the dirt floor. 'Worst piece of luck I ever had in my life, gettin' tangled with that hold-up. Last thing I wanted was to meet Bourdell again.' There was a pause as he shifted again, a thud and a curse, then a deep indrawn breath.

'Guess I'd best tell you the whole thing. I used to be a locksmith, long time ago. But I got a weakness for playing poker. There was this gambling man, a clever sonofabitch who took me for more money than I was ever likely to have in my whole darn life. I owed him so much I was never gonna get free. Fact was, I was close to ending up dead in some alley with a knife in my back. Figured I had no choice when this man offered me a deal. All I had to do was open a safe. Inside a bank.'

'Alicia told me,' Garvin said. 'The robbery went wrong, and you ended up in jail.'

'Yeah.' Again Hollick was silent for a long moment, his breathing loud as he squirmed closer. 'You ever been in prison? It was bad. Once I was free I swore I'd stay out of trouble. But the past has a way of catchin' up with a man. I'd met Bourdell inside, though he was using another name then. He broke out of the pen, six months before I was released. I hoped I'd never see him again, but about a year ago he tracked me down. Wanted me to help with a robbery. He'd got details of the safe, all he needed was a man who could open the door.'

'You turned him down?' Garvin hazarded.

'Sure. And I managed to lose him, but not before I'd met his two sidekicks, Towse and Whip. I tell you, I was scared; Bourdell's bad enough, but those two gave me nightmares. I spent months lookin' over my shoulder. Then my luck changed. I won a heap of money in a poker game, and for once I managed to hang on to it. I owed my brother close on three hundred bucks, and I figured I'd give him the surprise of his life by payin' him back. I knew he'd be at Dobie's Bluff for the rodeo, and I had money to spare, so I took a chance and booked a seat with Wells Fargo.'

A series of muffled thumps and laboured breathing told Garvin that the man was making progress. 'I didn't recognize Whip, not until we were at the way station. He'd got me spotted though, said he'd kill me if I tried to make a run for it. There was an old guy, a drunk. He got wind somethin' was wrong, threw himself out of the coach. Almost wished I'd had the guts to do the same. You know what happened to him?'

'He got away,' Garvin said, 'but not for long. Somebody killed him a week or so back. Since Towse was dead by then it must have been Whip or Bourdell.'

142

Hollick grunted. 'Guess they'd have found me too. Listen, Garvin, I'm real sorry about your sister. I didn't see much of the hold-up. Towse knocked me out cold the minute I stepped out of the coach. I didn't come round until it was going dark. Me and Simons were tied up, lying across two of the horses from the stage. It was Simons told me that Whip an' Towse had killed your sister, took her off someplace, along with the driver an' one of the passengers.'

It was getting hotter. Sweat was pouring down Garvin's back, and his head was throbbing in time with the fiery agony pulsing through his body. 'You anywhere near yet?' It was an effort to force the words from his parched throat.

'Halfway, maybe a bit more. Hold on. Reckon you know the rest of the story. Towse and Whip spent hours with Simons, every place we stopped. Whip hardly seemed to sleep at all . . .' Hollick broke off. 'Don't reckon I'll ever forget that man's screams, not for the rest of my life.'

'Some memories never leave a man,' Garvin replied bleakly. He would never be free of what had happened to his sister. 'Though if you don't get a move on that might not trouble me much longer.'

'I'm coming.' Hollick said breathlessly. After a short while he went on. 'Once Bourdell was sure we'd lost the posse he brought me out here. I guess you'll think I'm yellow, but I stayed put, just like he told me. Then Al arrived, and it wasn't just about me any more . . .' his voice trailed off. He didn't speak again, though Garvin could hear him still making his agonizingly slow progress across the dirt floor.

There was no way to measure time, but the air inside the hut grew ever hotter. Hearing nothing but faint sounds of movement and an occasional pained grunt from

Hollick, seeing only the dancing motes of dust in the single shaft of light, Garvin drifted in and out of consciousness, his body so racked with pain that he would have welcomed Whip's return, if only it brought him a few seconds of relief.

CHAPTER EIGHTEEN

The sun beating down on the metal roof was making it as hot as hell. Garvin's throat was dust-dry and his tongue had swollen so that it felt too big for his mouth, though he barely noticed. Nothing seemed able to distract him from the pain in his tortured muscles, which ran like a fire through every part of his body. An indefinable sound roused him briefly, reminding him that there was a reality beyond his own suffering. Not knowing whether hours or merely minutes had passed since he spoke to Hollick he formed words in his head and somehow forced them from between his lips. 'Where are you?' he croaked.

'Here.' Hollick rasped back. Something brushed against his boot. 'The knife. Is it that one?'

'Yes.' Garvin's mind was suddenly crystal clear. He had been waiting for this moment, dreading it. When he tried to swallow, his throat working, his mouth was too dry. 'I'll work my foot lower so you can reach the knife, you're only a couple of inches short.'

His body cringed, the knowledge of what he was about to do was almost too much to bear. 'Ready?' Garvin pushed on to his toes while he waited for Hollick's whispered response, then he let his legs buckle. A scream sounded in his head, but he never knew whether it escaped past his teeth. The grey space inside the hut turned black and spun into a bright shower of stars, the air so thick and hot in his chest that he thought he saw red flames flickering in the darkness, licking around his body. Remotely, as if his flesh no longer belonged to him, he felt Hollick's fingers busy at the top of his boot. An interminable age passed.

'I've got it.' Rollick sobbed at last. 'I've got it.'

Garvin was beyond making any response, though gradually he straightened his legs and took the agonizing weight from his shoulders, doing what little he could to relieve their pain. Whatever he did, it still felt like his back was breaking.

Time went on, each second a measureless torment. Garvin wasn't aware of the moment when Hollick at last cut through the ropes and set himself free. From a great distance he heard the man choke off a sob as he began to restore movement to his cramped body. More endless ages crawled past. There was a faint metallic jingle from close by.

Hands touched Garvin and he groaned in protest.

'Easy. Come on, I've got you.' The hut was spinning again, and Garvin closed his eyes, not wanting to fall, not wanting that terrible wrench on his arms again. Hollick lowered him gently to the floor, then turned away as Garvin laid his forehead in the dust, unable to stop the tears that ran silently down his face.

'I can't find anything strong enough to prise the links apart,' Hollick said huskily. 'There aren't any tools in here.'

Garvin was on his knees, staring into the darkness

towards Hollick, who was rooting around in a corner. 'What about that hole in the roof? Can't you make it bigger?'

'I doubt it. There's about a ton of nails holding them metal sheets on, I put 'em in myself last year.'

'We have to do something before they get back. Let's try the door again.'

'It's a waste of time,' Hollick said, his voice rising as if he was close to panic. 'I heard them drag that old stove across it, we'll never be able to shift that much weight from here.'

Garvin rose to his feet, staring at the roof only inches above his head. If he'd had his hands free he'd have been tearing at the rusted metal with his bare hands, though common sense told him it probably wouldn't have done much good.

'Hey!' Hollick came towards him, his fingers working at something cradled between his hands. He was prising the top from a cobweb covered jar. He threw down the lid and took a long swallow, then held the jar so Garvin could do the same.

The thick syrupy peach juice felt wonderful. Once the juice was gone Hollick doled out the peaches, holding Garvin's share to his mouth between his fingers. Finally Hollick licked out the empty jar as far as his tongue could reach. The two men grinned at each other, like boys engaged in some forbidden mischief.

'I was hoping to find a bottle of whiskey I lost track of a while ago,' Hollick admitted, 'but I reckon that was better.'

'Tasted pretty good,' Garvin conceded, easing his shoulders as much as the handcuffs allowed; the pain wasn't gone, but it was no longer a problem. He stood up and prowled around the tiny space. 'We don't want to be in here when Whip and Bourdell get back. How about we try pulling down this wall?'

'It might work if we had something to use as a crowbar, but there's not so much as a damn hoof nail in here.'

'Then we'd better come up with some kind of plan for dealing with whoever comes walking in on us. Bourdell's not stupid; by now he'll have worked out I was lying about Alicia heading for the Circle S. He'll be back.' Garvin went to the door. 'If you could just find something heavy, maybe I can bring Whip down, give you a chance to knock him cold.'

'There's this.' Hollick was still holding the jar. 'But if it's Whip that comes in, what about Bourdell?'

Garvin shrugged. 'One thing at a time. We . . .' he broke off. 'Listen,' he whispered.

They were silent, straining their ears as a soft rhythmic sound grew louder and clearer. 'Don't sound like a horse,' Hollick breathed. 'Could be an animal.'

'On two legs? Don't reckon you'd get bears around here.' Even as he spoke Garvin felt his heart lurch, some extra sense telling him the identity of the person who now stood silent outside their prison, or maybe he knew her so well that he could recognize the sound of her footsteps. 'The crazy little fool!'

'What?' Hollick stared at him.

'That's Alicia! Damn all stubborn, cross-grained females!'

'Al? It can't be. Why the heck would she come back?'

A voice came to them, high-pitched with anxiety. 'Uncle Tom? Cole? Are you there?'

Garvin closed his eyes. 'Ask her yourself,' he said hopelessly.

148

'Al, in here. Any chance you can get the door open?' Hollick yelled.

'Uncle Tom! Are you all right? Is Cole in there too?'

'I'm here, and we're both fine and dandy, now quit wasting time. For the Lord's sake, Al, answer the question. The door.'

'They've put that old stove up against it, I can't move it, it's too heavy. I'm sorry.'

'Never mind,' Hollick said. 'We need something that'll break through a chain. Go look in the house.'

'No!' Garvin protested. 'Alicia! Get out of here.'

'I won't be a minute,' she replied, her hurried footsteps fading.

'Damn you!' Garvin turned furiously on Hollick, glaring down at him, tugging at his shackled wrists in his frustration. 'Are you so all-fired concerned for your own skin that you'd take a chance on that maniac coming back and finding her?'

'Al won't turn and run, just on your say-so,' Hollick said. 'You should know her well enough by now to figure that out. Best we can do is try and get ourselves free, then maybe we'll have a chance of settling with Whip. I want to see that man in his grave. That's the only way to keep her safe, an' you know it.'

'She should have been safe already, dammit.' Garvin paced, two steps across the dirt floor and back again, a dozen restless turns before the girl returned. They heard her scrabbling at the door, a metallic clang as she hoisted herself on top of the old stove. A hand appeared in the hole near the top of the wall. It held a spike, the kind of thing used by railroad engineers, and a hoof rasp with a point at the end. 'That was all I could find,' Alicia said. 'I had a quick look to see if they'd left a gun, but there's nothing.'

'Those are just fine,' Garvin replied, as Hollick took the tools from her. 'Now you listen to me. Get back to your horse and go. Right now.'

'No, not until . . .' there was the sound of a quickly indrawn breath as she broke off. They heard her jump down, and the soft pad of her boots as she ran, then there was silence.

'Come on,' Garvin said urgently, turning his back and thrusting his manacled hands at Hollick. 'Get these off me, and make it fast.'

'Kneel down,' Hollick replied, 'I need the chain on the ground.'

'Don't waste time with the rasp, just prise a link open.' Garvin said, as he obeyed.

'I'm tryin',' Hollick said, 'hold still. The spike's too thick. I need somethin' to hit it with.'

'Use your damn head,' Garvin growled. 'Come on!'

There was the dull clink of metal on metal, and Garvin strained to pull his wrists apart as Hollick jabbed the spike down again and again. Suddenly he stopped.

'What's wrong?' Garvin said impatiently.

'Shut up an' listen.'

Garvin did as he was told, knowing now what had sent Alicia away. Several horses were coming, the thud of hoofs growing louder as the animals were ridden to the hitching rail outside the lean-to. Garvin found he was holding his breath as the creak of leather told him the riders had dismounted. There was a jingle of spurs and the heavy tread of boots crossing the yard.

'I'll go fetch Garvin.' It was Whip's voice, his tone eager.

'Not now,' Bourdell said curtly, 'see to the horses first. We're gonna need them, soon as Garvin's told us where to find the girl.'

'I just wanna take a look,' Whip protested. 'Won't take but a moment.'

Garvin swivelled to put his mouth close to Hollick's ear and whispered a few hurried words. The other man nodded, and moved cautiously to the side of the door, the jar that had held the peaches still in his hand. Exerting every ounce of his strength Garvin strove to force his hands apart, his shoulders straining. The manacles bit into flesh already raw and bleeding, but the chain didn't give way. Swallowing a curse Garvin gave it up and crawled across to where his knife lay on the ground, discarded after Hollick had set himself free. He leant back to pick up the weapon between fingers slick with blood, then pushed upright and backed into the corner opposite Hollick.

'Now,' he whispered. 'And make it good.'

'Water!' Hollick called hoarsely. 'Bourdell!'

They heard Whip laugh, then something heavy scraped against the wooden door. 'Hey, kinda dry in there is it? How 'bout you, big man, you got a thirst too?'

'I think Garvin's dead,' Hollick rasped. 'Ain't heard nothin' from him for hours now. For pity's sake, Bourdell, give me a drink.'

'You heard me, Whip,' Bourdell snapped. 'Leave 'im be. Put saddles on those spare horses an' tend the others while I load up with supplies. We'll take Hollick with us, Garvin too, if he's alive. We wasted enough time. I ain't missin' out on that payroll. If we can't find that girl before sunup tomorrow we're headin' north. Nobody's gonna go bringin' a posse after us on her say-so, not with Tate out of the way.'

Muttering, Whip moved away. Garvin flexed his arms, his fists clenched, the fingers of his right hand wrapped tightly round the hilt of his knife; he'd never tried killing a man while his hands were tied behind his back. He looked across at Hollick in the gloom, hardly able to make out much more than the glint in his eyes, and wondering if the man's nerve would fail him. If they'd only had a few more minutes. Without the chain linking his wrists, Garvin figured the odds would have been about even, but they daren't try again and risk being caught unawares; whoever stepped in through the doorway must be dealt with fast.

It felt as if they waited for hours. The air inside the hut was still chokingly hot, but the shaft of light coming through the hole in the wall was fading as the sun crept into the west. Hollick was hardly even a shadow, motionless, his hand half-raised. Eventually there were sounds of the stove being moved away, a man's muttered curses as he strained against its weight.

The door swung open and somebody stepped inside. All Garvin could see was a figure outlined against the brightness of the setting sun. He launched himself, throwing his whole weight forward, catching the man in the ribs with his shoulder and driving him to the floor. Bourdell's angry curse was bitten off as Hollick stepped in, his arm slashing down, the thick earthenware jar shattering in his hand.

CHAPTER NINETEEN

'Get his gun,' Garvin snapped. Hollick was standing as if he'd been turned to stone, his eyes fixed on the damage he'd done to Bourdell's head. One thick shard of pot was sticking out of the man's skull, while many more lay scattered in the dust, some of them splashed with red.

'You think he's dead?'

'Looks that way. Does it matter?' Garvin snarled. He butted Hollick's shoulder with his own. 'Come on, Whip might have heard something. Grab Bourdell's gun. And search his pockets, see if you can find the key to these damn things.'

Slowly, while Garvin fretted and kept an eye on the doorway, Hollick bent over Bourdell, fumbling to remove the six-gun from the sheriff's holster. 'I gotta tell you, Garvin, I ain't too handy with an iron. Even left-handed Whip's gotta be better than me.'

'Then hurry up and get these shackles off, and leave the shooting to a man who knows how.'

'Hey.' At a shout from outside Hollick froze again, his face blanching.

'Bourdell? Come on out of there, an' see what I found.' Whip sounded gleeful.

153

'Now what?' Hollick whispered. 'He's gonna wonder why he don't get an answer.'

'The key,' Garvin urged frantically.

Hollick was trying to push the gun into the belt of his pants. When he'd succeeded he turned Bourdell over and began groping in the pockets of his vest. 'Not there.' He fumbled with the button-down pocket on Bourdell's shirt, his hands trembling as he searched. 'I can't find it,' he said at last, forgetting to keep his voice down.

'Hey, that you, Hollick?' Whip called. 'What can't you find?' He laughed. 'If it's a key you're lookin' for, I got it right here. Figure you managed to take down Bourdell, so you maybe ain't so stupid after all. Guess that was a lie about Garvin, he's come back from the dead again, huh? Well, ain't that just fine. Step on outside, miracle man.'

Garvin gritted his teeth, seeing stars as he tried to wrench his wrists apart. 'You want me, you come and get me,' he said.

'I don't think so.' Whip laughed again. 'There's some-body out here just longin' to see you. Come on, honey, give your sweetheart a call.'

There was a muffled gasp.

'He found her.' Garvin felt his heart lurch. He had to get free. Hollick was still patting desperately at Bourdell's clothes; perhaps Whip had told the truth about the key. The man looked up, shaking his head.

'The gun,' Garvin whispered urgently. 'If I can distract him, give you a chance to get close . . .'

'I said, call him!' There was the crack of flesh striking flesh as Whip spoke, his amusement forgotten and his voice sharp.

'Don't come out!' Alicia shouted defiantly. 'Stay there, Cole, Uncle Tom. He's too much of a coward to come and

154

get you!' Her words were followed by a scream of pain.

'Come on, Garvin,' Whip repeated. 'Or you'll be hearin' more of that. Could be I'll put your little whore across my horse an' take her out where you won't find us. Bourdell told me that was your sister on the stage. She wasn't a lot of fun, reckon this one'll maybe make up for it.'

Garvin was shaking with fury. It was difficult to keep his thoughts under control, as his mind frantically turned over a hundred plans, not one of them worth a cent.

'You could take the gun,' Hollick whispered, offering it.

Looking at the long barrelled repeater Garvin shook his head; firing with his hands chained together behind his back, he'd be likely to hit Alicia instead of Whip.

Garvin pushed his knife into his belt so it was out of sight under his shirt, then stepped to the doorway. He found himself staring straight into the setting sun. A silhouette, bright-edged against the sky, stood close to the old adobe house. It had two heads, one a little higher than the other.

Whip laughed again. 'Hell, Garvin, it's good to see you again. I'm real glad you ain't dead. Lookee here. See what I found behind the woodpile.' He stretched out an arm, thrusting the girl forward. Alicia stumbled and almost fell, before he dragged her back to him again; the sun glinted redly on the knife he held.

'You're a big brave man, Whip Dooley,' Garvin said, his voice calm though his heart was pounding, his anger rising in his throat thick enough to choke him. 'Why don't you let her go? Every time I see you you're hiding behind somebody. Now you've lost your boss, and you've got nobody telling you what to do, so you're hiding behind a helpless kid.'

'I ain't hidin',' Whip growled. 'An' I ain't no fool. You think I'm gonna set her free when you got Bourdell's gun in your hand?'

In answer Garvin took a few paces forward then turned slowly around. 'No gun,' he said. 'And in case you hadn't noticed, I've still got my hands chained behind my back.'

'So Hollick's got the gun,' Whip's voice was suddenly strained. 'Hollick,' he called. 'You throw that damn gun out or I slit her throat. You gonna let your brother's kid die? Be a real shame to miss out on what I got planned for her, but I'll do it if I have to.' He pressed the knife harder against Alicia's neck. 'Don't keep me waitin' too long.'

'Garvin?' It was a whisper, a distracted murmur from the doorway behind him.

It would have been an impossible shot, even for a marksman, the girl shielding most of her captor's body. 'Do as the man says, Tom,' Garvin ordered.

There was a moment's pause, then something thudded to the ground off to Garvin's right. Whip gave a swift nod of satisfaction. 'Real sensible, Hollick. I sure hope you ain't done Bourdell no harm, 'cos he's the one who was keepin' you alive. Don't reckon you an' me will be raidin' no bank if he's dead. Go fetch him out here so I can take a look.'

'Always hiding,' Garvin said, a grim smile curving his lips. 'You don't have the guts to take me on, not even now. Come on, Whip, show us you're a man. You got a knife and I've got nothing. Why don't you step out from behind the kid and finish this?'

'No!' Alicia struggled in Whip's grasp. 'Cole, don't!'

'Guess you've got a good excuse,' Garvin went on relentlessly, 'what with me putting a slug in your shoulder, then the kid breaking your fingers. Maybe it's real hard, using that blade left-handed? Trouble is, Whip, from where I'm standing, it looks like you're a yellow-bellied coward who won't even face an unarmed man with his hands tied behind his back. You're wearing a yellow streak about a mile wide. What do you say, Hollick, that how it looks to you?'

With a roar of rage, Whip flung the girl from him, pushing her away so hard she slammed against the adobe wall, then dropped to the ground. In that split second Garvin almost lost the fight before it was begun. Seeing Alicia's head snap back as she fell he hesitated, and Whip Dooley had thrust his knife back into its sheath, his crazy eyes blazing, and his hand reaching for the gun he wore slung low on his hip, before Garvin had even begun to move.

Long legs pumping, Garvin raced desperately across the baked dust, dragging his gaze away from Whip's left hand and staring into the man's face, opening his mouth to let loose a wordless yell of defiance. He was aware of the gun, saw it rising as if in slow motion, heard the click as Whip thumbed back the hammer. There wasn't time to reach the man, all he could do was fling himself to one side, the world exploding in pain as his whole weight landed on one shoulder.

Right alongside his ear, the blast as the six-gun fired was deafening. With his head ringing and his senses adrift, Garvin wondered if he'd been hit. There was no time to worry about it. He rolled, got one knee to the ground and came upright, his feet taking him forward again without conscious thought, to send him barrelling into Whip. As his weight spun the other man around, the pistol's second shot cracked skywards. Garvin butted Whip in the face. They fell together, Garvin cursing as his wrists slammed against the shackles; he had tried instinctively to bring his

157

hands round from behind his back. There was no time to think, to plan his next move. Barely noticing as his head hit the ground, Garvin jerked his knee up to find its target between Whip's legs.

Whip fired for a third time, even as he went sprawling, a high-pitched scream escaping his lips. Garvin was helpless, unable to do anything but go after him and attempt to hold Whip down by sheer force of weight. Pitching himself on to the other man's body he hardly heard the pistol fire yet again, nor did he immediately feel the pain, only a jarring thud. Seconds later his side began to hurt, but the bullet had just grazed along his ribs; it was no more than a flesh wound. Even so, he couldn't win this fight. That didn't matter, as long as Whip didn't survive, but where the hell was Hollick?

Whip was struggling to push Garvin off him, blood gushing from his smashed nose. He couldn't take aim, since Garvin's weight was pinning his shoulder to the ground, so he used the gun as a club instead, bringing it smashing down on Garvin's skull.

Garvin had to roll away or risk having his head stove in. As he landed in the dust he flung himself flat, and heard a slug whine over his head. Bending his knees he lashed out at Whip, both boots catching the man's arm, delaying the inevitable for a few more seconds.

Whip's yelp told Garvin he'd done some damage, but Whip had learnt his lesson. He rolled to his knees, far more quickly than Garvin could manage, hampered as he was. Shuffling backwards on his knees, putting a couple of yards between them, Whip had time to sight down the barrel of the gun, an evil grin on his bloody lips. 'Your luck just ran out, Garvin. You're gonna be real dead this time.'

Garvin stared at eternity, ready to throw himself aside,

yet knowing he couldn't hope to move faster than the slug that would soon be coming his way.

'You're looking at the wrong man, Whip.'

As Garvin stared death in the face, the words seemed to come from some great distance, but that was an illusion. Tearing his gaze away from the hypnotic eye of the .45, he saw that Hollick had come. He stood with Bourdell's gun held steady in his hand, only two yards away. And he wasn't shaking any more. 'I ain't good with a gun, but at this range even I can't miss,' the wrangler said, his finger squeezing the trigger. With a speed Garvin could hardly believe, Whip moved, swivelling to bring his gun to bear on its new target.

The two shots came so close together it was impossible to say which man fired first. Without a sound Hollick fell, crumpling to the ground. Whip looked down at the reddened rag of cloth fluttering from his right shirt sleeve, laughing contemptuously. 'Nothin' but a crease,' he yelled triumphantly. The words were barely out of his throat before they were lost in a screech of pain. Garvin hadn't wasted Hollick's last stand. His boot slammed hard into Whip's elbow, shattering the joint and sending the six-gun flying from his hand.

Whip went scrambling towards the gun, whimpering, his bandaged right hand cradling his broken arm. Garvin went after him, groping for the hilt of his knife behind his back. He brought his hand as far to his side as the shackles would allow, turning, leaping, using his whole body to carry the weapon to its target.

The blade took Whip in the throat, Garvin's weight thrusting it deep. Blood spurted from the gaping wound, covering both men in a hot thick flood as they fell to the ground together. Whip choked, the sound giving way to an obscene gurgle as he drowned in his own gore. His right hand stretched in a last futile gesture towards the .45, then thudded lifelessly to the ground.

Garvin got to his knees, blinking furiously. Blood from a graze on his scalp was running down into his eyes. His head swivelling, he took in the scene of devastation. Alicia still lay against the wall of the house, but she was stirring, a little moan coming from her lips. Then she was looking at him across the dusty space, her lips trying to form words. 'Uncle Tom,' she whispered.

By the time Garvin reached Hollick's outstretched form the girl was beside him. There was a widening red stain on the man's chest. His eyes were open, roving from the girl's pale face to Garvin's, covered with blood.

'Whip was lyin',' he whispered. With a convulsive jerk Hollick moved his left hand, opening the fingers. 'All yours, Al,' he said, releasing the key to the manacles Garvin was wearing. 'Figure he'll take better care of you than a useless cardsharp.'

'You're not . . .' the words were choked off by a sob.

'You did just fine,' Garvin said. 'Thanks.'

Struggling for breath, Hollick met Garvin's look. 'Sure hope you mean to do the right thing by her.'

Moving his body round a little so he could reach the girl's hand, Garvin grasped it in his bloody fingers. 'Alicia, if you'll marry me I swear I'll do my best to make you happy. What do you say?'

Tears rolling down her cheeks, her eyes flicking from her uncle's face to Cole Garvin's blood-streaked features and back again, Alicia nodded.

Tom Hollick's face creased into a smile, then with a last rattling breath, he sank back to the dust.